THE PUZZLED PRODIGY

To Daniel. As God delivered your
namesake from the lions, may you also
trust God to keep you safe from harm
all your life. "No kind of hurt was found
upon him, because he had trusted in
his God" (Daniel 6:23). Thank you for
your boldness of vision.

THE PUZZLED PRODIGY

JEFFREY ARCHER NESBIT

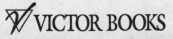

VICTOR BOOKS

A DIVISION OF SCRIPTURE PRESS PUBLICATIONS INC.
USA CANADA ENGLAND

THE CAPITAL CREW SERIES
Crosscourt Winner
The Lost Canoe
The Reluctant Runaway
Struggle with Silence
A War of Words
The Puzzled Prodigy

Cover illustration by Kathy Kulin-Sandel

Library of Congress Cataloging-in-Publication Data

Nesbitt, Jeffrey Asher.
 The puzzled prodigy / by Jeffrey Asher Nebit.
  p. cm. — (The Capital crew; 6)
 Summary: Thirteen-year-old Cally tries to help his younger
brother, a gifted child with learning problems, use his photographic memory to win the school spelling bee.
 ISBN: 0-89693-075-0
 [1. Brothers and sisters — Fiction. 2. Gifted children — Fiction.
3. English language — Spelling — Fiction. 4. Christian life — Fiction.] I. Title. II. Series: Nesbit, Jeffrey Asher. Capital crew; 6.
PZ7.N4378Pu 1992
[Fic] — dc20   92-23304
                                                           CIP
                                                           AC

 1   2   3   4   5   6   7   8   9   10   Printing/Year   96   95   94   93   92

VICTOR BOOKS
A division of SP Publications, Inc.
Wheaton, Illinois 60187

1

I should have known. Of course, I always say that. But this time, there's no doubt. The clues were all over the house, and I just missed them.

First, there was the dictionary Mom kept in our combination den/library/game room. Actually, it's just an old storage closet that we expanded a little. But it's the one room in the "barn"—besides our bedrooms, of course—where we can get a little privacy.

It seemed like every time I wandered in there, for days on end, the dictionary was open to a different page. The first couple of times, I just figured one of the twins—Karen or Jana—was doing a paper or something. I didn't think much about it.

Then there was the way my little brother John kept following our conversations so closely around the house, hanging on every word. Every once in a while, he'd take out this little pad he kept in his pocket, write something down, and smile.

In his room, which was easily the biggest mess I've ever seen in the history of messy rooms, I kept finding these scraps of paper with four-syllable words on them. Weird. Definitely, weird. But that was John. Though he was nine, he was so quiet that you could never quite be sure what was going on in his mind.

Then there was the long conversation John had with Mom about *antonyms* and *synonyms* one night.

They must have talked about antonyms and synonyms for close to an hour. I don't know why he didn't just ask his big brother. I could have told him in ten seconds. "Antonyms: words that mean the opposite thing. Synonyms: words that mean the same thing." End of discussion.

See, I'd make it simple like that because John's attention span isn't real long. He tries. He really does. But he tends to wander on to the next thing pretty quickly, for some reason.

But he paid close attention to Mom's explanations on this, which should have told me something. But it didn't. I just figured John had this thing about antonyms and synonyms.

For the next week, John drove us all crazy. Every time one of us would use a word, John would ask us what the antonym was. Or he'd ask us for a couple of synonyms.

For instance, a bunch of us kids were hanging out in front of the TV, just talking. "Well, that was ridiculous!" I said to no one in particular, gesturing at the TV screen.

"What's the antonym?" John piped up from across the room.

"Of what?" I asked.

"Ridiculous," he said.

"Not so ridiculous," I told him, chuckling. John frowned, so I scrunched up my forehead and thought. "I don't know, John. Normal? Ordinary?" John nodded, satisfied.

I had no idea if I was right, of course. I sort of knew what ridiculous meant, but I hadn't put a whole lot of thought into it.

He finally started making a list of antonyms. He started putting them down in a notebook, which he began to carry everywhere. The list got into the hundreds, and then into the thousands. He had antonyms everywhere. And I still had no clue why he was doing this.

Then I started to find books that were left open, with certain words circled. A day or a week later, I'd come across the same word, this time in our set of encyclopedias. I'd find one of the books open to that particular word.

Like "architecture." I saw it circled in a book, then I saw it again in the first book of our encyclopedia set — a description of what architecture was, complete with examples.

It had to be John. I was certain of that. He always did weird stuff like that, constantly rooting around in things, looking at things. He'd been doing it ever since he was two or three.

Then he started carrying this thesaurus around. We'd be talking, just horsing around, and then John would suddenly whip out his thesaurus and start to thumb through its pages.

Once, I asked him what he was doing.

"Nothin'," he replied sheepishly.

I knew he was looking up words. "You're doing synonyms, right?"

John nodded. "Yeah, I'm doing synonyms."

"But why?"

"No reason," he said, staring hard. He blinked and left. I didn't see the synonym book for a week after that.

Finally, after weeks of watching John go through all of this, I stumbled on at least the beginning of the answer to the mystery. It was late at night, close to bedtime. We'd all finished our homework and were watching some TV before bedtime.

Except John. He wasn't around. That wasn't a crime, and no one even noticed. He usually flitted in and out of our family gatherings like a ghost anyway.

I'd just ducked into the bedroom I shared with my 11-year-old brother Chris, up in the loft, and I was on my way back downstairs when I heard John's soft voice muttering something from his bedroom at the end of the hall.

Curious, I tiptoed quietly toward his room. His door was open a little, so I peeked in, careful not to make a creak or a rustle.

John was slumped over on his bed, reading something. I couldn't see what it was, so I just listened intently.

"Oh, phooey," John said with some disgust. "So what was Tigger doing, then?" He thumbed back through the pages until he found what he was looking for. "Oh, yeah. He was hungry." He turned back to another page and began reading again. Then he groaned and flipped back to yet another page.

It took me several minutes to realize he was reading from *The House at Pooh Corner*, A.A. Milne's classic book about Winnie-the-Pooh and Christopher Robin's other stuffed animals. It had been one of my little sister Susan's favorites. I'd read it to her a lot.

But what in the world was John doing with the book? He was much too old for it. I was sure he'd read it once upon a time. We all had. So why was he reading it now?

It took me another several minutes to catch on to what he was actually doing with the book. He was reading some part of the book, and when he was stuck on something he didn't understand or remember, he was going back and looking at what had happened earlier in the book to refresh his memory.

The only problem was that he was going back and looking a lot. An awful lot. For every page he was reading, I figured he was going back to earlier parts of the book at least five or six times. At that pace, he'd never finish the book.

John's hunt for antonyms and synonyms was tied up with this somehow. I was sure of it. I didn't know how or why—yet. But they were definitely linked. I'd just have to go about finding the answer carefully.

Because one thing was sure. If I challenged John, he might never answer. More than likely, he'd hide the book he was reading and never look at it again. John was like that. He kept his thoughts very private. I never knew what he was thinking. And he never volunteered anything. You had to ask John things. He didn't just tell you them on his own.

I left John to his struggle with the great Pooh bear and crept back down the hallway and descended the stairs quietly. Mom would know what was going on. She had to know. I'd ask her tomorrow.

I didn't get a chance to ask Mom about John's mysterious behavior at breakfast the next morning because she was cramming for a test that night. She was really nervous too. This was her first test in about a zillion years.

You see, Mom was going back to school at a college right around the corner from our house—George Mason University—so she could get the degree she didn't quite get when she was younger. My crummy father had ordered her to drop out of school when I was born, and Mom had never gone back.

Until now. My Uncle Teddy had pulled a few strings (like he always did somehow), and Mom would be able to take some courses in the fall and spring and get her degree by the following summer. She was getting a degree in International Affairs. All her courses were on junk like that. She was going to take her Foreign Service test after she'd gotten her degree.

But all that was in the future. If she didn't pass her first test tonight, then all her dreams would go up in a big puff of smoke. Poof. No career in the Foreign Service. Gone.

Karen, Jana, and I tried to cheer Mom up. We didn't have a whole lot of luck.

"Mom, remember all the advice you gave us about how not to worry too much going into a test because you'd like, you know, forget half of what you learned if you tried too hard?" Karen asked her over breakfast.

Mom looked up from the book she was studying between sips of coffee and glared at Karen. "Easy for you to say," she answered grumpily. "You didn't have to explain why we didn't cross the 37th Parallel during the Korean War."

"The what?" I asked.

"The 37th Parallel," Mom said evenly, glancing over at me.

"What in the world is that?" I pressed.

"It was . . ." Mom glanced down at the book. She rattled off the definition from the book, something about the world and geography and symbolic importance and the Communists and the Chinese and troop movements and strategic importance.

"Oh, I get it," I said at the end. "You mean, the other side drew a line in the sand and said, 'Step across this and we'll really get mad'?"

Mom smiled. It was the first time she'd smiled all morning. "Yes, Cally. That's what they did."

I beamed. "See? This international affairs stuff isn't so hard."

"Hey, Mom?" Jana chimed in. "Before my tests you always used to ask me, 'What's the worst thing that can happen to you?' The answer was always, 'You flunk the test and then you try harder on the next one.' Well, it's the same deal here, isn't it? I mean, there *will* be more tests, won't there?"

Mom looked over at Jana. "Yes, there will be more tests. But if I can't pass this one, which ought to be so simple, then I'm just wasting my time. I'm doing all this for nothing."

"Oh, Mom," I groaned. "You're not wasting your time. This is what you want to do . . ."

"But if I can't pass this dumb test—"

"You'll pass it. Don't worry," Karen said confidently. "You know that stuff cold. You probably know it in your sleep."

Mom sighed. "I don't know. I think I do. Then I try to remember something and I draw a blank."

"You're trying too hard," I said soothingly. "Just relax. It's just like tennis. If you try too hard, your muscles knot up and you can't hit out. It's exactly the same thing."

"Well, I'm not sure it's exactly the same . . ." Mom began.

"Sure it is," I offered. "There's no difference. Just don't try so hard. You know this stuff."

"Yeah, Mom, Cally's right," Karen added. "You know it. I'll bet you've read that book six times by now."

Mom glanced down at her text. "I have been over this several times."

"And you know it cold. Admit it," Karen said forcefully.

"Okay, already," Mom said, leaning back in her chair. "I give up. You guys win. I know this stuff cold, and I'm not going to worry about this test anymore."

"Great!" I said, pounding my fist.

"And if I fail, I'm blaming it all on you guys for giving me rotten advice," Mom grumbled.

"Gotta work," Jana said. "It always did for us. It'll work for you."

Mom nodded and then leaned back and started to look at something in her book again. "Mom!" I exploded. "What are you doing?"

Mom looked up sheepishly. "I just wanted to check one other thing . . ."

"Stop it," I ordered. "No more checking. No more

worrying. You're going to go to work today and forget about this test. You'll do just fine."

Mom took one more glance down at the book. "It's just the one thing," she protested.

"No," I said firmly. "Promise me you won't keep worrying all day long?"

"Promise, Mom?" Karen seconded.

Mom looked back and forth between the two of us. She knew she was outnumbered. "All right, I won't worry," she said. She closed the book and set it off to the side. "I have studied this. I should know it."

"You do know it," I said.

"All right, I do know it," Mom nodded. "I just have to trust that I'll remember it when the test starts."

I caught a funny movement out of the corner of my eye. It was John, who had followed every word of our conversation like he always did at meals. He just sits there and takes in everything anyone utters.

But this time, John had looked away. He was staring off into space, out the nearest window. Strange. That wasn't like him. Something was troubling him very much. There was something about what we'd just been discussing.

I'd have to ask Mom tonight. But then I remembered that Mom was at school tonight, and Aunt Franny would be here with us. I'd be in bed when Mom got back from her test.

So I'd have to remember to ask her tomorrow. I'd just have to remember to do that.

3

I promptly forgot to ask Mom about John, of course. Other things happened. My friend Elaine was driving me crazy at school. The state tennis championships were coming up, and I was trying to decide if it was a good idea to play doubles with Evan Grant or not. *And* I discovered where Lisa Collins' locker was.

I didn't try too hard to find out where Lisa's locker was. I happened to bump into her one day after school, and I walked her to our Bible study in the trailer just on the edge of the junior high school grounds.

The furor over our Bible study had calmed down a lot once we'd moved it to the trailer. The newspaper had done one final story, sort of on how it had all worked out in the end and how everyone was happy now. And that was that. No more controversy.

Which was just fine with me. I knew Elaine was kind of upset that it had all ended so soon. But I was happy beyond belief that the TV cameras were all gone and that the school had gotten normal again.

Once I knew where Lisa's locker was, it was weird how I somehow managed to find myself wandering down that hall. I didn't see her the first few times I walked past her locker.

And then on the fourth or fifth trip past it, there she was. Her reddish-blond hair had fallen forward, covering her face, as she twirled the tumblers on her lock. My legs got rubbery. My mouth got dry. My heart started to beat like a tom-tom. But I continued to walk toward her.

Lisa looked up when I was just a few feet from her locker. She tossed her hair back over one shoulder. Our eyes met, and she smiled at me. "Oh, hey Cally!" she said softly.

I nodded once. I tried to say something back to her, something smart and clever. Nothing came out. Absolutely nothing at all. The words, whatever they were, got stuck about halfway between my lungs and my incredibly dry mouth.

"Um," I finally managed to croak. "Hi, Lisa." I sounded like someone who's just thawed out after having spent the past few thousand years imbedded in a sea of ice at the North Pole.

Lisa smiled again. Boy, was it a nice smile. I'll bet she practices it. The teeth just showing a little bit. The eyes crinkled only slightly. A very sincere look to it. "Cally, I haven't seen you come down this hall much during the day. Where you headed? I'll walk with you."

I drew a complete, total blank. There was nothing there. A black hole had enveloped my witless brain. I had no idea where I was, which part of the school I was now in, or where I might be headed. The moon, for all I knew. I frantically tried to remember where I could possibly have been going to.

"The gym," I finally managed to squeak in the nick of time. When all else fails, go to something you know. And I knew the gym and the locker rooms. It had to be a safe haven.

"That's sort of on the way to my next class," Lisa said. "I'll walk with you partway." I started to move away from her locker, in the direction I'd come from. "Don't you want to go the other way?" she said, giving me a curious look.

My eyelids fluttered as I stopped and changed directions. "Oh, yeah. I forgot. I meant to go the other way."

Lisa moved in real close to me as we walked. In fact, she was walking so close that our arms touched as we moved down the hallway. I couldn't concentrate on anything. My mind was barely functional. I didn't see any of the other kids in the hall. It was like there were just two people in the entire world, Lisa and me.

"How's tennis?" she asked.

"Um, OK, I guess."

"You guys going to win state this year?"

"Probably. Who knows? We'll have to see."

"Who's number one—you or Evan Grant?"

"The coach alternates us, back and forth, depending on the number one at the school we're playing."

"What do you mean?"

"Well," I said slowly, thankful we were on a subject I knew well. Otherwise, it might have been the most idiotic conversation ever. "If their number one is a sneaky sort, who likes to get everything back, then I play number one because of my big serve and the way I charge the net. If their number one is a wild man, then Evan plays him."

"Oh, I see," Lisa said politely. "I guess it makes sense."

"Sure it makes sense. It's worked in every match so far."

Lisa nodded. "You see Elaine much?"

That one took me by surprise. "You mean, outside of Bible study?"

"Yeah, outside of that."

I thought about it for a second. I usually tried to avoid Elaine, she drove me so crazy. "No, not really. We talk sometimes. Elaine calls me at home sometimes to ask me about things."

"What things?" Lisa asked with a smile.

"Oh, I don't know. Just things. Nothing important."

"Like what?" she asked.

I sighed. "Like stuff from the Bible, I guess. What I thought about some idea she'd dreamed up after reading something from the Bible."

"Oh, that kind of stuff," Lisa nodded. She looked vaguely relieved, for some strange reason. I had no idea why, of course. "But nothing else?"

"No, not really. Why?"

Lisa shook her head. Some of her hair fell across my shoulder. I could smell her shampoo. "Just curious, that's all."

We walked in silence for a few moments. It occurred to me that I should ask her something. I didn't know what. But I knew I should ask her something.

"Well, I gotta go to my next class," she said, stopping at an intersection. "The gym's in the other direction."

"Yeah, I guess it is," I said, still not sure where I was in the school. I'd lost all contact with reality or where I was in the universe.

"So I'll see you around," she said, and started walking backward away from me. She didn't bump into anything. It looked completely natural, like she did that kind of thing all the time.

I started to back away too and tripped over the edge of the carpet at the entrance to the next hall. I recovered my balance in the nick of time. I waved at Lisa. She waved back. And then she was gone.

What was it I should have asked her? Oh, well. Too late now. I'd have to remember some other time. I started walking down the hall, turned a corner and kept walking. It wasn't until I was at the end of the next hall that I remembered where I was and that I was now almost late for my next class at the other end of the school.

What in the world was I doing wandering around in near-empty hallways, late to my class? I had no idea. Everything was a complete blur. A nice blur, though. A warm, fuzzy, glowing blur that made my whole body tingle.

The bell rang, and I about had a heart attack. I began to run to my next class, my mind racing for some excuse to offer up to my teacher. But the blur was still there. It was definitely still there.

The letter from the elementary school principal was on the dining room table a few days later, waiting for Mom when she got home from work. We all saw it when we got home from school. We knew, somehow, that it had to be about John. Not Susan. It had to be John.

Of course, I figured, it might just be a letter from the principal congratulating us on our successful move to Washington, welcoming us to the community. You know, nice to see you, hope everything's working out as you'd hoped.

Well, Mr. Principal, thanks for asking. We're doing just fine. Our family's getting along without our dumb, old dad. I wish we had one—a normal one, I mean. But we're doing fine. Really.

But then Jana said there was no way it was a letter like that. It had to be a "trouble" letter. The kind she gets from one of her teachers every so often.

"Yeah, it's prob'ly that kind of a letter," Jana nodded as we stared at it on the table.

"You think?" I asked.

"Sure," Jana said. "Look how nicely Mom's name is typed on the front of the letter. John's in big-time trouble, I'll bet. Let's open it and see what it says."

"And how do we explain it to Mom, that we opened the letter?" I frowned.

"She'll never know," Jana said with a wry smile.

"How's that?" I asked.

"Easy. We can steam it open, then put it back in the envelope when we've read it."

I gazed at my sister, incredulous. "How do you know how to do that?"

Jana shrugged. "I've done it before. It isn't hard."

I just shook my head. Jana was only a year younger than me, but seemed a *lot* older sometimes. "I don't believe it, Jana."

"Hey, it's not that big a deal. You just boil some water and stick the envelope in the steam . . ."

"But it's wrong," I said.

Jana snorted. "Oh, you and your Bible stuff. You think everything's wrong."

"But this is wrong," I persisted.

"Why?"

"Because it's about John, and we can't just go snooping around . . ."

"We don't know for a fact that it's about John," Jana said quickly. "It might be about something else."

"We should wait until Mom gets home, let her read it," I said reasonably.

"But what if she doesn't tell us what's in the letter?"

"Then she doesn't tell us."

Jana crinkled up her nose. "Oh, you're no fun."

"But I'm right. You know I am."

Jana picked up the letter, held it up in front of the light, and tried to read what was inside. It was a long, typewritten letter. That was about all I could see.

Jana tossed it back on the dining room table. "Yep, it's trouble. I can tell."

"How can you tell?"

"Because no one takes the time to write such a long

letter if they're saying good things about you. If you're doing great, they just give you decent grades and smile a lot at the parent-teacher conferences."

"You think?"

"I know," Jana smiled, then turned on her heels and walked away, leaving the letter behind.

I forgot about the letter after awhile, mostly because Chris managed to get me outside for a game of football. It was really starting to get cold, much colder than I was used to in Alabama.

But once we were running around, doing patterns and stuff, I forgot about the cold. And the letter.

When it got too dark to see the football anymore, I hit Chris with a really long bomb, and he just ran in the house with the football without saying a word. Boy, he was weird sometimes.

He bonked me on the head just as I walked through the door. "I'm gonna kill you," I muttered as my head recoiled.

"Can't catch me," Chris said, tearing for the stairs to the loft.

But I was too quick for him. I caught one of his legs as he was diving for the stairs. I quickly pulled him to me and locked both of his arms behind him. "You're mine now," I said heavily.

"Let go!" he bellowed.

I pinned his stomach to the floor. His face was smashed into the carpet. I ground my knee into the small of his back. "How's that feel?"

"Great," Chris grunted. "I love it."

I applied some more pressure, leaning forward. "How about now?"

"Feels good," he hissed.

I leaned forward and applied even more pressure. "How's this?"

Chris answered by bucking hard, like a bronco. I'd shifted my weight too far forward. I'd gotten just a little too greedy. I went flying forward like a sack of potatoes and crashed into the carpet in front of Chris, nose first. I'd have a monster of a rug burn on my face.

Chris popped up to his feet quickly. "Vic-to-ry," he taunted, and then tore for the steps again. I was in no mood to chase him, so I let him go. The door to the loft slammed shut a few seconds later.

I rolled over and touched my face gingerly. *Ouch.* It hurt. I'd really made a mistake. I shouldn't have leaned forward so much. A big mistake.

The front door swung open. Mom hurried through, slammed the door behind her, dropped off her coat and her handbag, and then walked through the house, waving at us. She grabbed the mail from the dining room table, checked in with Aunt Franny in the kitchen, and then went upstairs to change before dinner.

When she came back downstairs a few minutes later, I could see from the troubled look on her face that something was quite wrong. Maybe she'd flunked her test. But that was crazy. I was sure Mom had done all right on that test. Then I remembered the letter from John's principal at school. That had to be it.

"What's wrong, Mom?" I said, trailing behind her into the kitchen. "Did you pass your test?"

"Oh, that," Mom said, dismissing the test with a wave of her hand. "It was easy. There wasn't a question on there I hadn't anticipated."

"So you passed?"

"Yes, I passed, Cally," Mom said. "I aced it, just as you and the other kids predicted."

"Hey, that's great! Then what's wrong?"

Mom sighed. "Oh, just things."

"Anything I can help with?"

"Not really," she said with a small smile. "But thanks for asking, Cally."

"Mom?"

"Yes, Cally?"

"Is it that letter? Is that what's bothering you?"

Mom's head jerked around. She stared at me, hard. "What do you know about that letter?"

I blinked. "Nothing. I promise. It's just that Jana guessed it was trouble, that's all."

Mom looked at me for the longest time. Aunt Franny was in the other room, saying good-bye to the other kids. It was just the two of us, Mom and me. "All right, Cally. I'll tell you what. I need your help on this. Can I trust you to keep this to yourself? Are you old enough?"

I nodded fiercely. "I am, I promise."

"Okay, then, after Timmy, Susan, and John are asleep tonight, we'll talk. All right?"

"Sure."

Mom walked over to me and gave my arm an affectionate squeeze. "Thanks, Cally. This will be hard. I'm glad I can count on you."

Then she left the kitchen quickly, to see Aunt Franny out. And I stood there, wondering what I'd gotten myself into.

I didn't pay much attention to TV that night. Not that I ever do anyway. I've never gotten into zoning out in front of the TV, like Jana does all the time. It's like eating a bag of potato chips. You eat and eat and eat, then you wonder why because they don't fill you up at all, and they're pretty lousy for you too.

I don't know why I was so nervous about having this talk with Mom. Maybe it was because I was worried about John, though I wasn't absolutely sure that was what the letter was about. Maybe it was because I could see how Mom was so troubled by it.

And maybe it was because, for the first time since Dad had left, Mom was turning to me for help. This was something for Dad to do—or, at least, something a normal dad was supposed to do. But our dad wasn't normal. He was a drunk, and he ran out on Mom. So there was just me.

I still had lots and lots of anger toward Dad. I wasn't sure it would ever go away, no matter how much I asked God for help, no matter how many times I prayed for him at night as I was going to sleep.

The raw anger I felt toward him was always there, always just on the edge waiting to leap into my mind. Why? Why did he do it? Why was he so selfish? Why was he so mean to Mom? Why did he have seven kids and then abandon them, like they didn't exist?

I knew I would never get the answers I wanted. Not ever. But I still asked them, over and over. And I would keep asking them, because I knew that it would always affect me, that I would grow up and be the kind of dad he never was.

Mom came down the stairs after she'd tucked Susan in bed and said good night to John, took two coats from the closet and tossed mine over to me. "Let's go for a walk, Cally," she said to me.

"Mom, it's freezing outside," Jana said, glancing away from the TV for just a moment.

"I feel like taking a walk anyway," Mom said.

"You're crazy," Jana said, and then turned her attention back to the TV again.

Mom just smiled. "Jana, honey, you have finished your homework, haven't you?"

"Sure, Mom," she answered without looking over.

I almost started laughing. When Jana wouldn't look you in the eye, that was a surefire giveaway that she had something to hide. In this case, no doubt, it was that she hadn't finished her homework.

Mom had a rule, and she was very strict about it— on school nights, no TV until homework was finished. Karen and I always lived up to this, Chris mostly did, but Jana was always a tough call.

"Jana, do I need to ask Karen about this?" Mom asked.

I could see Jana sigh to herself. She hated it when Mom called her on stuff. Karen would know whether Jana had finished her homework. She knew everything Jana did. Not that Karen would rat on her twin sister. But it was about all Mom could throw at Jana.

"Mom," Jana pleaded, "I'm almost finished. Really. I just have a few more math questions and one history chapter. That's all. I can read the chapter on the bus tomorrow, and I can do the math questions during homeroom. I promise."

This time I did start laughing. "Ha," I said.

Jana scowled at me. "This is none of your business. This is between Mom and me."

"I was just curious, though," I said nonchalantly. "Which one of the zillions of conversations you have on the bus and in homeroom were you going to give up to do your homework?"

"You keep out of this," Jana said angrily. "This is none of . . ."

"Jana!" Mom said insistently, cutting her off. "You're right. This is none of Cally's business. This is our business. And I'm telling you to turn the TV off right now, go back upstairs, and finish your home-work. We both know that if you don't get it done now, you never will. So get going!"

"But, Mom, I'm halfway through this show, and they're about to . . . "

"Go!" Mom said forcefully. "Right now!"

Jana jerked up and popped the TV off like she'd been hit by lightning or something. "All right," she said grumpily. "But I wish you'd just trust me. I told you I'd get it done."

"Jana, honey, I do trust you," Mom said easily. "But I also know how incredibly difficult it is to get things done on a bus or in a homeroom where kids are yell-ing and talking."

"I can do it, though," Jana pleaded one last time.

"Go upstairs, Jana," Mom sighed.

She trudged past us, but not without a parting shot at me. "Thanks, you traitor," she muttered under her breath as she passed by me. "I'll get even."

"Ooohhh, I'm worried," I shot back.

"You'd better be," Jana tossed over her shoulder

and then bolted upstairs before I could answer back.

"Don't ride her too hard, Cally," Mom said to me when Jana was out of earshot. "She tries hard. She really does."

"Yeah, I know. But there's no way she's gonna get anything done during school. There's just no way. Kids hang all over her all day long, she's so popular."

"I know," Mom agreed. "That's why she has to get things done before she goes to school."

I put my coat on and began to move toward the door. "Let's roll."

Mom put her coat on, and then reached in the closet again for a hat and gloves. She grabbed some for me and tossed them over. "Here. It is cold outside."

It took me a second to get used to the blast of cold that descended on us as we moved outside. I clapped my hands together and stomped my feet to get the blood circulating. Mom just scrunched up.

"You sure we shouldn't talk inside?" I asked.

"No, I don't want the other kids to hear this," Mom said somberly. "So this is the only safe way."

We began to move toward the road, where a few streetlights illuminated the landscape.

We walked along the path next to the road for a couple of minutes without saying anything. I knew Mom would get to the letter in her own time. It was obvious something was worrying her a lot, and she didn't know what to do about it.

"Cally, do you think John is stupid?" she asked me finally.

"John, stupid? No way. He's strange about some things. He does things differently. But he's definitely not stupid."

"So you think he understands what you're talking about when you explain something to him?"

I thought about that for a second. John was quiet. He almost never spoke unless he was spoken to. You could ask him for something from a page he'd read, and he'd have the answer in an instant. But did he understand what he was reading or what he was hearing?

"Mom, I don't think John's stupid," I responded. "I really don't. He understands things in a different way, that's all. He has a tough time seeing how one thing leads to another, or how two things connect."

"But you don't think he's stupid?"

"No, I don't. I can see how he might struggle in school. He remembers so much from what he reads, it has to, you know, sort of overwhelm him. But he's definitely not stupid."

Mom nodded as we continued to walk along. "I see it that way too. John is so unique. His gift is so unique. He just doesn't know what to do with it."

I thought back to all the dictionaries and encyclopedias, and the time I'd seen John struggling with *The House at Pooh Corner.* It was falling into place for me.

"You know, Mom, I think I can figure out what's going on."

"You can?"

"Yeah, sure," I shrugged. "All these antonyms and synonyms and stuff. John's trying to figure out what everything means. He reads it and remembers it. But he hasn't quite figured out how to make it all mean something."

"And?"

"And I saw him trying to go through that Winnie-the-Pooh book the other night. He'd get through a paragraph or two, then he'd have to go back to another page just to check on what he should have known already."

"Really? You saw John practicing like that?"

"Sure. He didn't know I was standing in the hall. And it was, you know, like he has all these pages spread out in front of him, and he can't connect the story that runs through them. He needs to learn how words turn into sentences and then into paragraphs and then into chapters."

Mom stopped and stared at me. "Cally, that is very perceptive. I'm impressed. I really am."

It was a good thing it was dark, so Mom couldn't see me blush. "Oh, come on. You just have to look at John and you can see how he's trying to work things out."

Mom clasped her hands in front of her. "I wish it were that easy."

"But, Mom, it *is* that easy."

"Not according to his teachers at school, it isn't," Mom said quietly. "They're all giving up on him. They don't know what to do."

"Is that what the letter was about?"

Mom nodded. "Yes, it was from the principal. They want John held back a year. They want him to go into remedial education."

A chill went through me. "He's flunking?"

"Yes, he's flunking all of his classes but one."

"Math? He's doing OK in that class?"

"Yeah," Mom sighed. "He hasn't missed a question in math yet. But he's flunking everything else. And the teachers don't know what to do about it."

"So they want to put him in special ed? How come this didn't show up before?" I asked. John had always done OK before. Not great, but he hadn't flunked.

"It was all rote memory stuff before. Not compre-hension or intuition or inference. That's what the prin-cipal and the school psychologist are guessing."

"What?"

Mom laughed. "I mean, he did fine when he just had to remember something from a page he'd looked at. He struggles when he has to explain what it actually means."

"Oh, I see."

"So do you have any ideas?"

"Me?"

"Yeah, you. Carl Lee James, direct descendant of the infamous Jesse James. Do you have any suggestions?"

I thought about it. "How about a tutor, at home?"

"How do we pay for it?"

"Maybe the school would pay for it."

"Hmm, maybe. We can certainly ask. Any others?"

"We can start working with him at home. You know, ask him questions, get him thinking about things."

Mom nodded. "That's good too. But it won't help right now. They want to move John immediately."

"You can't do anything about it?"

"I have a conference with his teachers, the principal, and the school psychologist the day after tomorrow. Like to come to it?"

This time I knew the chill that swept through me wasn't from the cold. This wasn't for me. I was just a 13-year-old kid. I couldn't handle this. This was for Mom and Dad. This was their job, not mine.

But then I thought about John, and how lost he probably felt right now. And then I got mad. Real mad. So mad I couldn't even see straight. Somebody had to look out for him. It might as well be me.

"Sure, Mom, I'll come along with you," I said finally.

Mom reached over and gave me a quick hug. "Thanks, kid. I knew I could count on you."

I started to work with John the very next morning. There was no time to lose. We had to work fast.

I tossed the newspaper, *The Washington Post,* in front of John as he sat down for breakfast. "Hey, John, check out the story on that new movie they're making up in New York, and how they turned on all the fire hydrants and flooded a few blocks just so they could get a good shot."

"What story?" John asked, giving me a blank stare.

"It's on the front of the 'Style' section of the paper. You'll see it."

I watched John as he fumbled through the paper, which he usually didn't read. He pulled that section of the newspaper out and looked at the front for a second.

"This one?" he asked, pointing at a story about a movie being shot on location in New York City.

"Yep. That's the one."

John was silent for a moment as he read. One of the reasons I'd picked that story was because it "jumped" from the front of the section to the inside of the paper. John would have to remember what he'd read on the front as he turned to the inside of the paper to finish the story.

I could see that he was struggling. He had to go back to the front a couple of times to get everything, even though the story was short.

"Pretty wild, isn't it?" I asked him nonchalantly.

"Yeah, I guess."

"You remember the guy they're talking about, don't you?"

"Which guy?"

"The little kid, the movie actor they're talking about in the story. He was in that movie you liked so much this past Christmas."

"Oh, yeah, that guy," John nodded. "I liked that movie."

"And isn't that pretty amazing, what they have to do just to make a movie?"

"I guess they have to," John said vaguely.

"How much do you think it cost them?"

John stared at me for a second. "To do what?"

"To turn on all those fire hydrants and flood all those streets."

John nodded. "Oh, that. Well, um, isn't water free? Maybe it didn't cost them anything?"

I laughed. "No, water isn't free."

"You mean we pay for water?"

"Sure. We pay something."

Now John was interested. "How much do we pay?"

I shrugged. "I don't know, maybe a couple of pennies a glass."

John thought for just one second, maybe two. "Wow. Then it cost those guys about $150,000 for that one part of the movie."

I sat back in my chair. "How'd you figure that?"

"Easy, glasses into gallons, then I figured how many gallons it took 'em and multiplied," John said proudly.

"I see," I said, nodding. "So did you figure in the snow?"

"Snow?" he asked, knitting his brow.

"Yeah, it snowed on the last day they were shooting. Did you figure that into your equation?"

John gave me that blank look again. "Um, no, I sort of forgot that. But snow wouldn't add much. It isn't very dense."

"And snow is free," I added quietly.

"Oh, yeah, I forgot," John said. "So it wouldn't have added anything to the cost."

"Right."

John fidgeted in his seat. This kind of grilling made him uncomfortable. It probably made him really uncomfortable in school. When he was doing something he was good at, like figuring, he was fine. But otherwise, he clearly struggled.

John flipped to the front of the newspaper. He stared hard at a story on the front of the newspaper. It was about autistic kids and how people had suddenly "discovered" all of these wonderful things about them, that they weren't really stupid. In fact, the story said, some of them were practically geniuses once they'd figured out how to help them communicate with the world.

"That's a neat story too," I told John.

"Yeah, I can see that," he mumbled as he continued to stare at the story.

Neither of us read the paper usually. Only Mom does. But I'd looked at it this morning before I'd tried my little experiment out on John. And John was only staring at it now to avoid me.

But I could see that he was actually reading the story on these autistic kids. Then I could see that he was getting even more into it, the more he read.

"Hey!" he said excitedly when he was about halfway through it. "This says that this one kid had been banging into walls and falling all over himself and drooling and junk, and that everybody thought he was a real moron. And now . . ." John paused, read some more, then shook his head. "Now it says he can write poetry and that he's really smart."

I'd already looked at the story, so I knew what it said. But I prompted John anyway. "So how'd they figure all that out?"

"Easy. Somebody figured out that if they held their hands, they could type out what they wanted to say on a computer."

"Type it out?"

"Yeah, with one finger. They hold their hand, and then they type each letter with one finger."

"And that one kid can write poetry now?"

"All the time, this story says. And there are other kids who can do all sorts of things."

I could see that John was really impressed by the story. But did it mean anything to him? "So sometimes kids can be really smart, but no one around them understands it?"

John shrugged. "Sure, I guess."

"Know anybody like that?"

He grimaced, thinking hard. "Not really."

I just nodded. I didn't want to press this too hard. "Well, anyway, you should read the paper more often, John. There's all sorts of interesting junk in there."

"But there's a lot of *boring* junk in there too."

"So skip those parts." Then I had a brainstorm. "Hey, I'm curious . . ."

"I'm John, glad to meet ya," he answered without looking up.

My jaw dropped. That was a game that Karen and I played all the time. We'd catch each other like that. But you had to be quick. And John had never played before. "Pretty good," I finally muttered. "You got me." John only smiled and kept eating, so I continued. "So I was thinking, you know, what if you had this really hard problem, how would you go about getting an answer?'

"What?" he asked, looking up.

"You know, if you had to find an answer to something, how would you go about it?"

"Like what?"

"Beats me. I was just wondering, like, if maybe you had to read through all sorts of stuff to get your answer, how would you go about it?"

John gave me the strangest look. "I'd read everything. What'd you think?"

"And you'd remember it?"

Now he was really staring at me. "Yeah, I would."

I could see that I wasn't getting through. Sure, John remembered everything he read. But in no particular order, without any rhyme or reason. Now, I just had to make him see that, somehow.

John suddenly pushed his chair back from the table. He crammed two more bites in his mouth and then got up to leave. "You're gonna be late to school, Cally."

"I know," I sighed. "I'm always late."

"So why don't you get up earlier?" he asked me.

It was a reasonable question, of course. Without a reasonable answer. "I just can't," I mumbled.

"Sure, you can. Just set your alarm clock back."

"But then I wouldn't get as much sleep in."

John shook his head. "You're weird."

"I know."

John started to fidget, like he wanted to say something and leave, all at the same time. "You know, I really wish it was that easy," he said finally, gazing off into space.

"You wish what was that easy?" I asked, not totally sure what John was talking about. He had a habit of doing that, changing gears and going off in a direction only he understood.

John still looked away. "You know, figurin' stuff out. I wish I could do that."

"You do? Why?"

"Because then I could help Mickey figure out what was wrong with Mark, that's why."

I frowned. "The twins, you mean?"

"Yeah, them."

Mickey and Mark Landis were identical twins. They were the only friends John had in the world, the only kids I'd ever seen him playing with since we moved up to Washington. John was such a shy kid. He kept to himself so much it made it tough to find friends.

But the twins were big-time model airplane buffs. John liked that kind of stuff too. He liked going through the diagrams and putting all the pieces together, so it made something whole when he was finished.

John would have the twins over for the night, and the three of them would sit up in John's room the whole evening, just putting these model airplane kits together. They'd skip TV, popcorn, ice cream, whatever.

But, now that John mentioned it, I hadn't seen Mark in the past few weeks. Mickey had come by once, maybe twice. But not Mark.

"So what's the deal?" I asked John.

"Oh, Mark's sick. He's been to the hospital for all these tests, but they can't figure out what's wrong with him."

"Tests? What kind of tests?"

John still didn't look over at me. "Oh, they keep

looking at his blood, counting things in his blood. You see, he's real tired all the time. He throws up a lot, he gets dizzy, and he has to take naps. He's missed a bunch of school."

"And they're testing his blood?"

"Yeah, Mickey says they're testing his bones too, the stuff inside his bones, you know, the . . ."

"His bone marrow?"

"Yeah, that stuff."

An uncontrollable shudder swept through me. My throat got tight. He had leukemia. Mark had leukemia. That's what it had to be. They just hadn't told Mickey yet. That's what it had to be.

"So what does Mickey think it is?" I finally asked.

"Ah, he doesn't know. He just says Mark'll get better once he's had enough sleep."

"Yeah, maybe."

When John finally glanced over at me, I could see that his eyes were brimming red. He was on the verge of tears. "So don't you see? If I could just figure it out, then everything would be all right. It would be OK. I could tell Mickey what the problem was, and then Mark would be all right."

I swallowed hard. "That'd be great, John. Someday, I know you'll be able to do stuff like that. Someday."

"Yeah, sure," he said bitterly.

"John, trust me," I tried again. "You'll do it."

John just slammed his hands against his legs, nodded once to himself, hard, and then turned to leave. "Gotta go to school," he mumbled.

And then he was gone. He was always doing that. He walked out on you in the middle of conversations, like he'd forgotten he was having one. I wondered what it would take to change all that. I hoped it wasn't flunking out of the fourth grade.

I can't remember when I'd ever been this nervous.
Not for the national indoor tennis championships. Not
when we'd first moved to Washington, D.C. Not even
when I'd first thought about maybe asking Lisa Collins to go to a movie or something.

Mom was a wreck. I could see that. She'd been a
wreck the entire morning. She'd barely managed to
make it through breakfast.

In the end, she'd decided not to tell John that we
were going in for a conference with the principal and
his teacher. I don't know why she didn't tell him, really. Maybe she figured she could do something about
the situation, and that she'd never have to tell him
anything.

I figured it was hopeless. They were going to hold
John back and that was all there was to it. Teachers
were like that. But I'd given my word to Mom that I'd
go to the conference with her. So I'd taken the morning off from school. Mom had taken a half day of leave
from work.

So why was I so nervous? I don't know. Maybe,
somewhere inside where I wouldn't admit, I secretly
hoped that we could do something. I had no idea
what. But something.

Mom didn't say much on the way to the school. She
just held on to the steering wheel of the car for all it

was worth, like maybe if she let go we'd go careening off into oblivion.

"Mom, it'll be all right," I finally said as we neared the elementary school.

"Do you think?" she asked without looking over at me.

"I know it will," I said reassuringly. "God will take care of John. You know that."

Mom almost smiled. "And what about us?"

"I think we're lost causes," I snorted.

"That's what I was afraid of." But she smiled this time. A little one, but a smile nevertheless.

For she knew I was right. God would take care of John, just like He took care of everyone who had some sort of a problem. He never let anyone suffer extraordinarily. He always looked after those who couldn't look after themselves.

But that still didn't help my unbelievably dry cotton mouth as we made our way to the principal's office. My insides were churning as we walked along the empty corridors of Thompson school.

There were two young women waiting in the outer office as we arrived. One of them stood up and offered her hand to Mom. She had wispy brown hair that just touched the collar of her plain dress. She wore almost no makeup at all, I noticed. "Mrs. James?" she asked. Mom nodded and took the hand that was offered to her. "Hi, I'm Nancy Travis, John's teacher."

Mrs. Travis turned to the other woman in the office, a tall, striking woman with brightly painted fingernails, short-cropped black hair and a tailored suit. She contrasted so sharply with John's teacher that I found myself glancing back and forth between the two involuntarily.

This second woman stood up and offered her hand

as well. "I'm Dr. Sheryl Burnley, the psychologist for the county's school system. I've had a chance to review your son's file and observe him in class. I've also spoken to him briefly."

I could see Mom stiffen at that. She shook the lady's hand, politely. But it had shaken her, the thought of some psychologist looking at her son without her permission.

Mom turned to look at Mrs. Travis. "Is that standard practice, to observe kids in class? And to question them without a parent's permission?"

"Oh, I didn't question him, Mrs. James," Dr. Burnley offered quickly. "I would never do that without your permission."

Mom looked puzzled. "But you just said . . ."

"That I'd observed him, yes, I have done that. And that I'd had a chance to talk to him a little. But it was only briefly, as he was leaving the classroom. He stopped to talk to Mrs. Travis here, and we had a little chat."

"About what?" Mom asked coldly. I could already see that this wasn't going to be a whole lot of fun.

"Just things. Nothing important, really," Dr. Burnley answered with the most professional smile I'd ever seen.

"You said you've reviewed his file as well?" Mom asked. "So what did you find?"

Mrs. Travis stepped in quickly. "Why don't we wait for the principal? We can go over all of this in the conference."

Dr. Burnley looked over at me. "You must be John's oldest brother, Cally? Is that right?"

I stared at her, wondering how she knew who I was. "Yeah, that's right. But how'd you know my name?"

"I've looked at John's file," she answered with a grim smile. "Remember?"

"Oh, yeah," I muttered.

Fortunately, the door to the principal's office opened before it got any more awkward. A stooped, elderly man filled the doorway. He gestured for us to join him.

"Welcome, Mrs. James. I'm Robert Murray," the principal said to Mom as she walked into his office. "And welcome, Cally," he added, taking my hand as well as I walked past him into his office. It was a surprisingly firm handshake.

There were four seats gathered in a sort of semi-circle around his well-organized desk. I took a seat at the end, Mom sat beside me, Mrs. Travis sat beside her, and Dr. Burnley took the seat at the far end. We all waited for the principal to open things up.

"All right, OK, well, then," Mr. Murray said as he settled into his well-worn leather chair behind the desk. I wondered how many of these things he'd been through in his life. Zillions, probably. He looked down at the file on his desk. He rifled through some of the papers before looking up. "Mrs. Travis, why don't you bring us up to date on the situation here?"

Mrs. Travis glanced over at Mom and me quickly. Mom acknowledged her with a curt nod. I just fidgeted in my seat. I was beginning to wonder desperately why I was here. This all seemed pretty adult—much too adult for me.

"Well, as we all know, John has done quite well with his math," she said, just plunging right in. "He has right from the beginning of the school year. He has a real aptitude for math. It's really in the other subject areas that he's struggling. And it's starting to get much worse. He's beginning to fall quite far behind the rest of the class."

"Why is it, do you think?" Mr. Murray asked.

Mrs. Travis shrugged. "I don't know. I've tried some different things. I can't spend a great deal of individual time with him, of course, because I have the other students in the class. But from my limited time with him, it seems as if he loses track of things. He gets to one point in something, and he can't remember what preceded it. There's no connection from one thing to another."

"But he's fine with his math?" Mr. Murray asked.

"That's right," Mrs. Travis nodded. "As long as he has the problem right there in front of him, he just solves it. It's when he has to remember how one thing leads to another, when he has to reach a conclusion about something, that he has problems."

The principal turned to Dr. Burnley. "Is that consistent with what you've observed?"

Dr. Burnley nodded. "It is. And with John's file as well. His rote memory is fine, as is his problem-solving. It's the logic sequence where we have the problem, which explains why it's only showing up just now."

"Why now?" the principal asked.

"It's really not until now that we begin to ask our kids to make the leap from what they've read to what it means. Until now, they merely had to remember it. Now, they have to understand it and relate to it as well."

Mom looked down at the floor. I could see that she was really struggling with this. I was sure she was wondering where she'd failed, what she'd done wrong.

"Hey, you all know about John's photographic memory, don't you?" I asked timidly.

All three of them looked over at me. "His what?" Mr. Murray asked.

"You know, his photographic memory," I repeated. "You know about that, right?"

Mr. Murray glanced at the other two. "Do we?"

The psychologist shook her head and looked to Mrs. Travis. "He does remember things rather well," Mrs. Travis said softly. "But I can't say I've noticed . . ."

"He remembers *everything*," I said rather loudly. "You mean you haven't noticed that?"

Mrs. Travis stared hard at me. "John is very quiet in class, Cally. He doesn't say much, either to me or to the other students. All I have are his test scores to go by and, right now, he's failing in everything but math."

A chill settled on the room. I could feel it. I was sure everyone else could too. But I couldn't believe this. They didn't know John had a photographic memory? How could they not know that? How? It was so obvious.

"If John does, indeed, have that kind of recall," Dr. Burnley said slowly, "it would explain why he's so adept at math. It might also explain why he's struggling with the logic sequencing."

"Why would that be?" Mr. Murray asked.

"Oh, when someone remembers everything like that, the books say they sometimes have trouble sorting through all of that information. It's like a computer that gets overloaded with too much information. It all spills onto the screen in no particular order. That may be what's happening to John."

Mom finally spoke up. "So what can we do about it?" she said, her voice quavering from the combination of fear and anger I was sure she felt.

Mrs. Travis folded her hands in her lap. "Well, perhaps special remedial classes for the remainder of this year, to bring him up to the fourth-grade level, and then a repeat of normal fourth grade next year. That could do it."

"No!" Mom said loudly, her voice almost echoing in the small room. "He can't repeat fourth grade. That would be too hard on him."

"But, Mrs. James, we've done all we can," Mrs. Travis said, trying to meet Mom's gaze. "We only have so many resources. This is a public school, after all. We can't spend all our time tutoring just one student."

Mom looked down at her lap. I could see that she was doing everything she could to keep from crying. "Isn't there anything you can do? Anything you can try?" she asked, her voice almost a whisper.

"No, I'm sorry," Mr. Murray said. "Really. Remedial education would be best. And then we'll see from there."

"But he's not stupid," Mom persisted. "And he's not retarded . . ."

"We know that," Mrs. Travis said. "But he does have a problem, which needs to be corrected."

Mom looked up, wild-eyed. "And how am I supposed to solve that problem? How do I do that?"

Dr. Burnley glanced over at the principal. "Perhaps with more specialized attention, which he'll get in a remedial education setting, his mind will orient itself to the task of remembering the order of things."

"And if he doesn't?" Mom asked.

"Let's just see first, Mrs. James," the principal said soothingly. "First steps first, OK?"

8

I knew Mom was devastated by the news that John was failing school. But what I didn't know was how John would take it. John was so quiet. He kept to himself so much, it was hard to figure how he'd take something like this.

Mom made all the kids leave the house when she told him. Even me. We all took a walk for about a half-hour. When we came back, John was sitting in front of the TV, watching some dumb show. Like nothing had happened.

"So?" I asked Mom, out of John's earshot.

"He didn't say much," Mom answered grimly. "He just nodded and said he'd try to do better. I told him to listen to his teacher in his new class. And he said he would."

"That's it?"

"That's it, Cally."

I shook my head. Like I said, John was hard to figure. Who knew what wheels were now turning inside his head?

I lay in bed for a long time that night, thinking. What would John do now? What would happen to him?

I wanted to help him in the worst way. But I had no idea how. It all seemed so hopeless. How can you make someone learn? How can you help him understand how to connect the dots in life? You can't. That's the answer. Or, at least, I couldn't.

Maybe someone else could. Maybe there was some teacher who could unlock his brain. Maybe.

In my own, rambling way, I prayed for John that night. I asked God to help guide John toward the answers that I couldn't find for him. I asked God to teach him like no one else could at this point.

I don't know how long I'd been asleep when I heard the door to my room creak open. Hours, maybe, or only minutes. The light from the hallway spilled into my room. A shadow drifted across the doorway, and then glided toward my bed.

"Hey, Cally, you awake?" a small voice asked.

It was John. I rubbed one eye. "I am now. What's up?"

John stood beside my bed, motionless. "I was thinking."

"About what?"

John pulled something from behind his back and held it up in the dim light. "This."

I leaned closer to see what he was holding. It was a copy of the Spelling Championship "Official List of Words." I'd seen John studying that before. "So what's up with that?" I asked him.

John set his jaw. "I want to enter. I know I'm only in the fourth grade, but I figured now they wouldn't mind."

"Why'd you figure that?"

"Now that I'm a moron, I figured they'd let me do anything I wanted. At first, I decided that I just wanted to drop out of school. I still do. But I also figured Mom wouldn't let me. So maybe I can do this instead."

I swallowed hard to keep the tears from coming.

"John, you aren't a moron. You know that. You just have to figure a few things out, that's all. And you aren't dropping out of elementary school. You can't do that."

"Will you help me get in the contest?" John asked, ignoring what I'd said. "Will you?"

"Sure, of course. You know I will."

"Will you do it tomorrow, so I can start practicing? They already have the winners in the fifth-and sixth-grade classes. The school championship is next week, in the auditorium."

"I'll go by first thing in the morning, before I go to my own school. All right?"

John nodded. I couldn't see his face, with the light streaming in from the hall behind him. "Thanks, Cally." He turned to leave.

"Hey," I said.

John turned back. "What?"

"So do you need help practicing? That is, if I get you in?"

"Yeah, sure, that'd be great," John said, a little enthusiasm creeping into his voice for the first time.

"OK, it's all set," I said with more confidence than I felt. "I'll get you in the contest first thing in the morning, and tomorrow night we start practicing."

"I've been practicing already, you know."

I swallowed hard again. "I know that, John. Now go get some sleep. We'll start tomorrow."

John turned and left the room as quietly as he'd entered. The door to my room closed again with a small "swish." Well, I had my answer. Now, it was my turn to make it happen.

I cut my last class and skipped tennis practice the next day to help John. I know it was wrong to cut class. I know that.

But I'd given John my word. And I would follow through, no matter what. I was ready to jump off a mountain for him right now. And the only way to get to John's school before all the teachers left was to cut class and race from my school to his on my bike. So that's what I did.

I got to Thompson just as school was letting out. I felt stupid wandering the halls, looking for the office of that psychologist, Dr. Burnley. But I just kept plodding on, asking the occasional kid for help. Which, of course, did no good. Nobody knew where her office was.

Finally, in desperation, I just made a beeline for the principal's office and asked one of the receptionists. "Why, it's right around the corner, son," one of them beamed.

I could feel my face grow flushed and hot, so I mumbled my thanks and bolted around the corner quickly. You know, sometimes I wonder. Why don't I do the obvious? Why don't I take the shortest path to things? Why do I make everything so ridiculously hard?

There was even a nice, neat sign on her door. So easy. Oh well. I knocked on the door softly. "Come in,"

a muffled voice called to me through the closed door. I
eased it open and slipped in.

Dr. Burnley was sitting, reading, behind her desk as
I entered. I glanced around her office quickly. It was
just like her—neat, ordered, everything in its place.
The bookshelves were brimming with big, thick
books. Her desk was mostly clean, with a few files
laid out on top carefully.

She looked at me directly as I entered. Gathering
my waning courage, I gazed back at her directly and
tried not to flinch. It wasn't easy. This lady scared me
a little. "Dr. Burnley, do you have a sec?" I said, trying
not to let my voice squeak. I only partly succeeded.

"Yes, yes, of course," she said, smiling. It was a
smooth, practiced smile. I'd seen that kind of a smile
before. Jana did it all the time. She'd sit in front of the
mirror, practicing her smile for hours. She had it down
pat, now. She could turn it on and off whenever she
liked.

And so could Dr. Burnley. It was a frightful thing to
see. Like a mask. I wondered what was behind that
mask. A real person, someone I could talk to? Or
something else?

I stepped inside the door awkwardly. I didn't know
whether to sit or stand. "I, uh, well . . ." I muttered.

"Please, close the door. Have a seat," she said
quickly, obviously sensing my uneasiness.

"Thanks," I said gratefully. I eased the door shut
and then sat down as quickly as I could.

"Now what can I do for you, Mr. James?" she asked
me with that professional smile of hers again.

"You remember me?"

"Of course I remember you, Cally James. You have a
rather unusual name. But I've taken a special interest
in John's case, as well."

"You have?"

She reached over and pulled a thick file out of a stand on her desk. She placed it in front of her. I could see John's name typed across the top. "Since our last meeting, I've had a chance to go over your brother's file more closely. It is a very interesting file. He is an interesting young man."

"You think?"

"Yes, I think," she offered without any trace of a smile. "A most unusual young man. His test scores are quite revealing. I don't think I've ever seen anything quite like it before."

"So what'd you find?"

Dr. Burnley opened up the thick file and thumbed through some of the papers. "Well, to be honest, what I found is someone who hasn't quite figured out how to harness all the knowledge he so obviously possesses."

I tried not to smile. Really. I tried hard, but I just couldn't hold it back. "Didn't I try to tell you that before, in that meeting? I told you he remembers everything . . ."

Dr. Burnley held her hand up, checking me. "Yes, yes, you did tell us that. And now that I've had a chance to go over things a bit more closely, I am inclined to believe you."

"Don't just take my word. Ask anybody who knows John. He's always been this way."

Dr. Burnley nodded. "Sometimes that kind of home learning doesn't show up in school, Cally. Some kids are totally different at home. They become someone else at school."

I nodded, though I wasn't sure I understood. I was the same everywhere. I just sort of plowed forward— at school, at home, on the tennis court, anywhere.

"OK, well, that's great, I guess. I'm glad you can see that. Because I wanted to ask you something."

"Shoot."

I looked down. A funny thought careened through my brain. *Don't think, Cally. It's like a second serve in a tight tennis match. Don't think about it too much, psyche yourself out. Just do it. Just take that step. Don't worry about the consequences.*

"Um, well, I had this thought about something that might help John," I said.

"OK, how can I help?"

I looked up, then, and took a second look at Dr. Burnley. She was still the same imposing woman. She was wearing another tailored suit, different from the one she'd been wearing before. She still scared me a little bit. Yet there was something . . .

"Why?" I blurted out.

"Why? Why what?"

"You know, why would you help me? Why would you help John?"

"Because that's what I'm paid to do," she said, turning on that professional smile. "I'm paid to help people, Cally. That's what I do."

I knew there was something else. I was sure of it. But I'd have to find it another day. I didn't want to get too far off the track right now. "Oh, well, never mind. What I was wondering was if you could help John with something. We talked about it last night. And John's been practicing. I just know . . ."

"Cally!" she said softly, stopping me. "How can I help you? What would you like me to do?"

I nodded. "OK, see, there's this spelling bee championship, at Thompson, I mean, coming up next week. It's for the fifth- and sixth-graders, the champions of each class. And John's in the fourth grade, so I was thinking, you know, that maybe John could enter it too. It would help him right now. I know it would."

Dr. Burnley leaned forward slightly. I could see that she was intrigued with the idea. "And you'd like my help? You'd like me to talk to the principal, Mr. Murray, to see if we can't arrange to let John in as a special entrant? Is that it?"

"Yes, exactly."

Dr. Burnley nodded. "You know, it *would* help John focus on his innate talents. It could help him with other areas as well. Yes, yes, it is a quite good idea."

"So you'll help?"

"I'll help," Dr. Burnley nodded curtly. "I give you my word."

"And you think it's possible John can get in?"

Dr. Burnley smiled. It looked just a little out of place on her. "Yes, Cally, I think it's possible. Everything is nearly always possible."

10

I just never seem to catch a break. They slapped me with detention for cutting my last class. Never mind that it was all for a good cause. Never mind that I had a nice, noble purpose. Someone ratted on me, and I got detention the next day.

Oh well. If John gets into the spelling contest, that's all that really matters, I thought glumly as I sat in the room with all the other kids who'd messed up for one reason or another. I stared at the clock on the wall and watched the second hand move around slowly.

I'd failed to bring anything with me to detention, so I was forced to play games. I'd already folded up a piece of paper into a triangle and played tabletop football with myself. I'd won, naturally.

Now, I was trying to see how long I could hold my breath. My all-time record, set during an unbelievably boring history class where we were studying the American Revolution, was a minute, fifty seconds. Some day I'd reach the two-minute mark.

I was about a minute in when Lisa Collins walked past the detention hall and spotted me. She slowed down as she walked past, peeked in the room, and caught my eye. She waved. I waved back. It was almost like she was looking for me. But that was crazy. Absolutely crazy. Why in the world would Lisa be looking for me?

I exhaled quickly, so Lisa wouldn't see what I was doing. I glanced back at the clock. Only a couple of minutes left in detention. I'd have to bolt from the detention hall to tennis practice. Everybody else would be out on the courts practicing by now. I'd only have a few minutes to change out of my street clothes and get out before practice actually started.

Lisa gave me another little wave, almost as if she was beckoning to me, and then disappeared from sight. The second hand on the wall clock moved slowly, slowly around twice. When the bell finally rang, it actually startled me a little. I jumped out of my seat like I'd been shot.

"Hey, Cally!"

I whirled in mid-stride as I was beginning to run down the empty hall toward the gym. It was Lisa. She'd waited for me.

She'd waited for me? Why would she do that?

"Oh, hi, Lisa," I muttered. I shifted from one foot to the other uneasily, anxious to be on my way. I would definitely be late now. Coach Kilmer wouldn't be happy. Today was the day we began to start working on doubles teams for the regional and state championships.

"You on your way to tennis practice?" she asked, moving quickly to my side.

"Yeah, and I'm sorta late."

"Oh, well, I'll walk with you then."

"Great," I nodded. I began to walk toward the gym. Lisa moved with me. She walked right beside me, brushing up against me about every other step.

Lisa glanced over at me shyly. She kind of peeked out from behind her hair, one eye covered by her bangs. "Would you mind if I watched practice a little? I've never seen the tennis team."

I almost stopped walking. But I knew that would be stupid, so I managed to keep one leg moving in front of the other. "Yeah, sure, no problem. But, um, like, why would you want to watch a practice? Why don't you come to one of our matches?"

Lisa smiled. I somehow managed to notice that her teeth sure were straight. "Oh, I'd really like that, Cally. Thanks for inviting me."

I looked away. Wait a minute. I was confused. Had I just invited Lisa to one of my matches? Was that, like, a date? I figured I'd better get this straight. "Well, sure, you know, you can always go to the tennis matches for free. They have stands right outside the fence you can sit in."

"When's your next match?"

I thought for a second. "We have one in two days, this Friday. It's against a school from Maryland. A pretty good team. They'll probably make it to the state championship in their state. I'm glad they don't play in Virginia."

Lisa nodded. "But you'll beat them?"

I shrugged. "Oh, yeah, sure, probably. Between Evan and me, we usually win pretty easily. If Evan and I start playing doubles together, that's three matches we'll always win. Then we just need one more from the other guys."

"So you're going to play doubles with Evan Grant?"

I looked over at Lisa. How did she know about Evan Grant? "I don't know. I haven't decided. I'm not sure Evan would like that."

"Oh, I'm sure he will. He really likes you a lot, Cally."

"He does? How do you know that?"

"Because I asked him."

"You did?"

"Sure. I was asking him about tennis and stuff. And he said he really likes you, that you're a great friend."

"Evan said that?"

Lisa looked a little confused. "Yeah, why wouldn't he say that?"

Now, I was really confused. First, I had no idea why Lisa would be talking to Evan Grant about tennis. Or about me. And, second, I had no idea why Evan would tell Lisa anything like that.

Once, Evan and I had been bitter enemies. Evan had gotten me kicked off the tennis team my first year at Roosevelt. Then, I'd beaten him in the finals of the 12-and-under national indoor tennis championships. I just assumed we'd be rivals forever and ever.

But we did practice together all the time, especially at the indoor tennis club where I worked part-time and where he was a member. And we *had* talked just a little about playing together as a doubles team.

"So you really think Evan would want to play doubles with me?" I asked.

Lisa reached out and touched my shoulder affectionately. It was just a small thing, but my knees almost buckled. I was sure my face was turning deep crimson. "Cally, I know he'll play with you. Just ask him."

I swallowed hard. "OK, I will. It can't do any harm."

"Of course not," Lisa said confidently.

I didn't say anything for a little bit. "So you really want to watch practice today? You know, it's pretty boring. We just do drills and junk like that."

Lisa laughed. "Oh, I know. But my dad can't pick me up for a little while, anyway. My mom's doing something, and he can't get away from work."

"So you're killing time anyway?"

"Something like that. But, look, I was also curious."

"About what?"

Lisa's voice grew quieter, softer. "Well, I was think-ing that, seeing how the match is on Friday and every-thing, maybe we could, like, go out to McDonald's or something afterward. Get something to eat."

I almost said something about how the team usually went out after matches. But I caught myself. That wasn't what she was talking about. She didn't want to go to some restaurant with the rest of the team.

She wanted to go with me. Just me. The two of us. Like, on a date. With no one else around.

"Um, sure, we can do that," I said, trying not to stammer. "I can probably get my mom to pick us up or something."

A big, bright smile burst across Lisa's face. "Great! It'll be fun. Maybe we could even go to a movie after that. There are some new ones I haven't seen yet."

"I'd have to check with my mom," I said quickly.

"You don't think she'd say no, do you?"

"Oh, no, no, I can do stuff like that. No problem," I said. I didn't want her to think I couldn't do this.

We arrived at the gym. I kept walking into the en-trance just in front of me, like I always did. Lisa stopped. "I can't go in there," she laughed.

I looked up stupidly. Then I spotted the sign that said "Boys Locker Room." I rolled my eyes. "Oh, yeah, I guess you can't."

Lisa gave me a short, little wave, her hand cupped. "I'll see you on the court. Ask Evan about doubles. I know he'll say yes."

I nodded somewhat numbly. "OK, I will."

As I turned away from her and disappeared into the locker room, it finally hit me. Lisa had asked me out. On a date. I was going on a date. This Friday. With Lisa Collins. Now, how in the world did *that* ever happen?

11

Lisa had been absolutely, dead right. Evan agreed to play doubles right away. He said he'd been thinking about it for a long time, and that it was the right thing to do.

In fact, he said, he thought we should play doubles together that summer as well. Because we were both going into the 14-and-under that year as 13-year-olds, we might do better at the nationals as a team against the boys who were a year older and bigger. I told him he was probably right.

And that was that. Evan Grant—once my enemy and chief antagonist—was now my partner. We were friend and partners. How strange it seemed.

Yet it also seemed fitting and right. The Bible said we were to forgive our enemies. What was it the Lord's Prayer said? "As we forgive those who trespass against us"?

Trespassing against us. It was a funny phrase. I guess it meant we were supposed to forgive those who stepped all over us, who did us harm. Evan had certainly done that. He'd deliberately gotten me kicked out of school for three days—and off the tennis team—once upon a time.

But that was all gone. Everything had changed since then. Evan had changed. I had changed.

It was funny, but I actually thought Evan listened to

me a little when I talked to him about God and the
Bible now. Just a little. Not a whole lot. Maybe just
with a part of his brain.

John started his remedial education classes. He
didn't say anything about it, as usual. He just started
going to the special class, with all the kids who had
trouble learning for one reason or another.

He only asked me once about the spelling bee. I told
him I'd talked to Dr. Burnley, the school's psychologist, who'd told me that she would try to help. He
didn't ask me about the conversation, or why I'd gone
to Dr. Burnley. He trusted me, I guess.

Dr. Burnley called me at home Thursday night, the
day before my "date" with Lisa. Actually, she called
just a couple of minutes after I'd hung up with Lisa,
who'd called me to ask if it was OK if her dad drove us
from McDonald's to the movie theater.

Jana really started to give me a hard time after I
hung up with Lisa. "Cally's going on a date! Big date!"
she started yelling to no one in particular.

I pointed a menacing finger at her as we squared off
in the living room. "Lay off. I mean it."

"Or?" she laughed.

"I'll do something," I glowered.

"Ooooohhhh, I'm so scared," Jana cooed.

"You oughtta be."

Jana started chuckling. "I can't believe it. You're
really goin' on a date. With Lisa Collins. Man, I just
can't believe it."

I started to get angry. "And what's so weird about
that? Huh? You wanna tell me?"

"Oh, it's just that . . ."

"What?" I almost yelled.

"Well, you know, Cally," Jana began gently. "It's
just that you never think about stuff like that. Going

on dates, I mean. I don't know how in the world you ever managed to ask Lisa out, that's all."

I didn't answer. I wasn't *about* to tell her that it was actually Lisa who'd asked—before I even knew what was happening. No way. I would never tell her that. I'd never tell anyone that.

Fortunately, the phone rang just then, before I really got myself in trouble. "I'll get it," I said quickly, cutting Jana off before she could bolt for the phone. I practically lunged at it. "Hello, the James residence," I managed to say calmly.

"Hello, this is Dr. Sheryl Burnley, from Thompson Elementary School. Is Cally James there, please?"

"Oh, hi, Dr. Burnley, this is Cally. What's up?"

There was no pause on the other end of the line. "I have great news, Cally," she said. "I've had a chance to speak to the principal. He's agreed to let John enter the spelling bee this year, as a fourth-grader. He agrees with me that the competition will be good for him, for his morale and self-esteem."

"Dr. Burnley, that's great!" I gushed.

"But, Cally, I have to be honest with you. I do have one concern."

"What's that?"

"Well," she said slowly. "What if John does badly? How will he take that, on top of what has already happened?"

I felt instantly relieved. "Don't even worry about it, Dr. Burnley. Really. This is something I'm absolutely sure John can ace. I know this is right up his alley."

"You're sure?"

"Yes, I'm sure. I know John. This is definitely something he can do."

Dr. Burnley sighed. "OK, I'm relying on you, Cally. I trust you. If you're telling me that John wants to do this, and that he can handle it, well, then I believe you."

"Believe me, Dr. Burnley, John can do this. I just know it."

"OK, well, then, the contest starts next Tuesday, after school in the auditorium. Will John be ready?"

I smiled to myself. "Yes, John will be ready. I'm sure."

"Very good," Dr. Burnley said. "Well, good night, then."

"Hey, Dr. Burnley?" I asked quickly, before she could hang up.

"Yes?"

"Um, I just wanted to say thanks. You know, for your help and everything."

"Just make sure John's ready, OK? Promise me that?"

"I promise. John will be ready," I vowed.

"Good," she answered. "Then that will be my reward."

I hesitated just a fraction of a second. "Will you be there?"

"At the spelling bee?"

"Yeah, there, at the spelling bee? Will you watch John, to see how he does?"

I could almost hear the smile that I was sure was on her face. "Yes, Cally, I will be there to see how John does," she said gently.

"Great. Thanks."

"My pleasure. Like I said before, this is what I'm paid to do. It's my job."

"I think it's more than that," I blurted out before I could think.

"Good-bye, Cally," she said curtly, cutting off any further speculation. "I'll see you at the spelling bee on Tuesday."

So we started the drills right away, that Thursday night, in John's room. It was just the two of us, John and me. I told Mom what was going on, but not the rest of the family.

Mom decided to let the rest of the "crew" in on it after we saw how well John did on Tuesday. No need to get the family in an uproar beforehand, she reasoned.

I was absolutely, completely, totally flabbergasted at how much work John had done already.

He'd studied phonetics. He'd learned about roots of words. He'd read and reread the little book they gave you with all the words for the spelling bee, along with the much larger book with additional words.

I guess that meant he really did have faith in me. He believed that I'd come through for him. He'd done all that work without knowing whether I'd be able to get him into the spelling bee.

It reminded me, in a very small way, of my own faith in something larger than myself. When I'd first started reading about Jesus, I had no idea who this man was who'd spoken so beautifully 2,000 years ago about some pretty interesting things.

Should I trust someone the Bible said was more than a man, the Son of God who'd died so that all the rotten things I'd ever done could be wiped off the slate?

That is, if I *believed* in Him and followed Him, if I had enough faith to reach out for something I wasn't entirely, completely sure was there.

That was faith. You had to extend yourself a little. You had to take that step out into the unknown. Would God be there to guide you, or would you drop into an unexpected abyss in the middle of the darkness?

John had taken at least one, small step. He was ready for that spelling bee. And, boy, was I in Dr. Burnley's debt. I can't even say how crushed John would have been if she hadn't gotten him into the bee.

"Okay, John," I said from one corner of his bed. "Let's go over the rules again. OK?"

"Sure," John answered. His glasses were drooping just a little on his nose as he sat curled up against two pillows on the other side of the bed.

"All right. When it's your turn on the stage, they give you the word. You don't have to answer right away. If you're not sure about it, you can stall a little by asking them to repeat the word. And then you can ask them to use the word in a sentence."

"Why do you do that?"

I thought for a second. "OK, think about a word like, ummm, like 'capital.' How do you spell it?"

John's eyes got wide. "Oh, that's right. There are two of those, one with an 'a' and the other with an 'o.' I get it."

"So you ask them to use the word in a sentence."

"Like?"

"Like, I tell you, that we're going to the Capitol today, how's it spelled?"

John closed his eyes for a moment. "I remember from one of my history books, that when you go to the Capitol, it's spelled . . . with an 'o.' Is that right?"

I smiled. "Yep. You've got it. Actually, with that word, it's almost always spelled with an 'a.' The only time it's ever spelled with an 'o' is when they're talking about the actual building itself, either the state capitol or the Capitol where the Congress is."

A worried look crossed John's face. "You know . . ." he began.

"What, John?"

"Well, I was thinking, you know, what happens if I get a word that can be spelled either way like that and I don't know what it means, or what either of them mean? How do I know which word is right?"

I sighed. "That will be the hard part. You'll just have to stall by asking them to repeat the word, use it in a sentence and, while they're doing that, you try to think about seeing it in a sentence like the one they're talking about."

"That's hard. I don't know."

I gave John my very best steely gaze. "You can do it, John. Don't worry."

John nodded. His glasses drooped a little further. "I'll try."

"Good," I said confidently. "Now, let's run through a few words . . ."

It astounded me to go over words with John. He knew them all. He had that little book entirely committed to memory. Every, single word. If there was anyone left standing on the stage, they'd have to go to the extra book with the extra words. And maybe even to the big dictionary, with every word in the English language.

Could John memorize the dictionary? Could he do that? I had no idea. If he made it past Thompson to the state championship, he could start working on the dictionary.

I wasn't even going to think about the national spelling bee championship they held every year here in Washington. We'd wait on that, see how things went. I just wanted John to get through Thompson unscathed.

After 45 minutes of drilling John on words and uses, I finally gave up. He'd exhausted me.

"John, you know this stuff cold," I said, shaking my head in wonder. "You'll kill 'em on Tuesday."

"You think so?"

"I know so. Don't worry about a thing. Be relaxed. You'll do just fine."

"What if I go blank, if I just forget everything?"

"That isn't going to happen."

"But what if I'm standing up there, and I get so nervous that I suddenly can't remember the words I can remember now?"

I thought about my tennis again. "John, in a really big tennis match, when I have a second serve I just have to get in? Well, sometimes, I get this thought in my brain that maybe I can't remember how to do it, how my arm works, how I hit the ball and spin it into the court?"

"Yeah, I guess."

"When I start to think like that, I just remember all the times in practice when I got it *right* and then I remember that if I've gotten it right in practice so many times, there's no reason in the world I can't get it right this one time in a match."

"I see."

"So it's no different here, with words. You've spelled these words right so many times in practice, there's no reason in the world you won't get it right when you're standing on the stage."

"But what if I get scared?" John persisted. "You

know, with all those people in the crowd and stuff?"

"Just forget the crowd is there," I answered. "That's what I do. I just look at my opponent and the umpire in the chair, if there is one for the match."

"So who do I look at?"

"You look at the judges. Never take your eyes off of them. Look straight at the judge who's giving you the word."

"Just like that? It's that easy?"

"Yes, John, it's that easy. Don't even think about anything else. It's just you, the judge, and that word. That's all you have to think about."

"But what if . . ."

"John!" I half-shouted. "You're thinking too much. You *know* these words. Trust your own mind. When it comes time, your mind will do what it's supposed to. But only if you don't think so much and get all messed up because you're worrying."

John started to nod. I could see that he understood what I was saying. *Now if he can only do it when he's on that stage,* I thought, *we'll be home free.*

13

I can't believe I was so nervous. My hands were so cold with sweat I had to rub them back and forth a zillion times. It still didn't help much.

My voice almost squeaked when I talked. I was in pretty rotten shape. My knees were buckling. I was having trouble breathing.

So it was a good thing I had my tennis match first, before I went out to McDonald's with Lisa. And it was a good thing that most of our "date" would be spent in the darkness of a movie theater where I wouldn't have to say much.

The tennis match was mostly a blur. At least, until we got to the doubles match. And then, thankfully, I got my head together.

Because, it turned out, the team we were playing really was quite good. There was no doubt in my mind that they would win Maryland's state championship. They had a couple of 15-year-olds playing first and second seed, and they were both very, very good.

Evan, who was playing second that day, easily won his singles match. I had a tougher time, playing their number one. The guy took me to a tiebreaker in the first set. I broke him once in the second set, though, and I didn't lose my serve. It made them both mad, though, and they kept trying to take our heads off with smashes during the doubles match.

This was the first time Evan and I had played doubles together. And, it turned out, ours was the pivotal match. Our third and fourth players had lost their singles matches quite badly.

I could see that one of our two doubles teams was winning rather easily at the end of the courts, while the other was getting creamed.

Which meant that Evan and I had to win our match. If we lost, Roosevelt lost. It wouldn't mean much to the Virginia tournament or the rankings going into it. But our pride was at stake. Plus, Evan and I wanted to play well together.

We'd never really talked about it much, not once we'd made the decision to play together. We'd gone about the task of figuring out how to play together separately. Each of us considered the other's strengths and weaknesses and decided how to play.

Evan was a tough, resilient, and endless baseliner. He'd sit back there and take balls behind the baseline forever. He could return them effortlessly—low, flat balls just a few inches above the net that almost landed three-quarters of the way back on the other side.

I was a sharp contrast. I attacked everything. I hit my serves hard and then came to the net almost immediately. My serve-and-volley was my greatest strength, with my crosscourt backhand perhaps a close second.

That backhand had saved me countless times. It was what kept the wolves at bay. Just when opponents thought they had me figured out, that they could lob me to death and keep me pinned down at the baseline, I'd murder a backhand crosscourt for a winner.

Together, Evan and I meshed pretty well. With me at the net and Evan playing deep, we could get to almost anything. Evan kept the ball in play. I went for the winners.

So, despite the fact that our doubles opponents were bigger and stronger, we prevailed in our match and Roosevelt won again. We were still undefeated going into the state tournament.

The match had been so intense—with Evan and me trying to figure out how to play with each other, when to switch, when to go back, when to charge the net together—that I had finally forgotten that Lisa was in the stands watching.

It was only after it was all over and we were celebrating quietly on the sidelines that I remembered. That's when the cold sweats and shaky knees set in.

I had no idea what to do. I didn't know what to talk about with Lisa. Did we have anything in common at all? Did she like sports? Was she crummy at math, like me? Did she have her own room at home, or did she have a whole bunch of brothers and sisters like I did?

It was weird, but I could talk to Elaine Cimons. No problem. Talking to Elaine was easy, like talking to Jana or Karen. Elaine was a friend, maybe one of my best friends. There was never a pause in a conversation. Elaine usually did most of the talking, but we always got along well together.

Lisa was another matter entirely. She was so pretty it took my breath away. Not that Elaine wasn't pretty in her own way. But Elaine had buckteeth, sort of. Or, at least her teeth hadn't quite figured out all the places they were supposed to be. And Elaine's body was, well, kind of geeky-looking. Like she hadn't quite grown into it yet.

Not Lisa. Her face was unblemished. Her hair was long and rich. Her clothes always matched. They always fit perfectly. She had a tan, even in the dead of winter, which Lisa told me once was because her folks took a vacation in Florida.

But what, exactly, could we talk about? I had no idea. It was a complete mystery to me. I'd find out, though. That was for sure, whether I liked it or not.

"Cally!" Lisa yelled to me through the chain-link fence that surrounded the tennis courts at Roosevelt.

I raised my head slightly above the row of players who'd gathered for high-fives just off one of the courts. I looked over at Lisa, who was waving to me now. I waved back, feebly, and swallowed hard. I tried to say something. A half-croak came out. "Hey!" I yelled louder, to make sure at least something came out.

"I'll meet ya!" Lisa yelled, inclining her head toward the exit from the courts. I just nodded back numbly, feeling very much like someone about to walk down the long hallway to his own execution.

Evan elbowed me in the ribs. "Yo, buckeroo!" he mocked me. "What gives? You goin' out with Collins?"

I just grimaced and gave Evan a baleful stare.

"Seriously?" Evan continued. "You've got a date with Collins?" Evan turned to the rest of the team. I could see he was about to announce my date to the whole, entire world. "Hey, guys . . ."

I tackled him before he could say another word. We both hit the court, hard. I scraped my arm, but I didn't care. At least he hadn't gotten the words out.

We rolled over once. "Not another word!" I hissed into his face through clenched teeth.

Evan rolled away and onto one elbow. He was grinning from ear-to-ear. "Man, you sure are nuts," he said.

"I mean it," I said again.

Evan popped to his feet again. I jumped to mine, as well. A few of the guys were giving us strange stares, wondering if a fight had started. "OK, OK," he laughed. "I won't say anything."

"Good."

Evan moved closer, so only I could hear him. "But how'd you do it? How'd you get somebody so hot to go out with *you?*"

I almost punched him. But then we probably would end up in a fight, as weird as I felt. It was like somebody had pumped me full of something. I felt like plowing through the chain-link fence or something.

I glanced over at Lisa. She'd moved away, toward the exit to the court at the other end. Apparently, she hadn't seen the commotion, because she was talking to a knot of people who were also waiting for us to leave the court.

"I dunno," I mumbled. "It just kind of happened."

"Just *happened?*" he said incredulously. "How do you mean?"

"It just happened," I said angrily. "That's all. We got to talking about maybe going out for something to eat after the match, and then about maybe going to a movie. That's all. It's no big deal."

Evan just shook his head. "No big deal? You are nuts. Collins is only the hottest thing in the whole school. I know guys who'd kill to sit next to her. And you just stumble into something like this."

"Hey, look, really. It's no big deal."

Evan gave me that smart-alecky, half-smirk of his, the one I used to hate but which I could now at least tolerate. "You know," he said slowly, "Elaine's gonna absolutely clobber you when she hears about this."

I clenched my fists. "Why would Elaine care? She's not my girlfriend or anything like that. We're just friends."

"Yeah?"

"Yeah. We just talk and junk. That's all. Elaine wouldn't care in the least about this."

Evan whistled. "Boy, are you dumb."

"You're out of your mind," I said angrily and started to storm off.

"Hey!" Evan said, grabbing my arm before I could bolt.

"Let go!" I said angrily, trying to jerk my arm free.

"All right, I will," Evan said soothingly. He eased his grip on my arm, but only slightly. "But I just wanted to say something."

"So say it."

"We were pretty good today, weren't we?" Evan said. I looked at his eyes. He really meant it. I could see that. And this was important to him.

"Yeah, we were," I answered, nodding. "We're a good team. I think we can do this."

"Me too," Evan beamed. He released my arm. "Now get. Your girlfriend's waiting."

"She's not my . . ."

"Just go, already!" Evan insisted.

I gave everyone else on our team high-fives before I left the court, grabbed my tennis bag with my extra racquet, and then began the long walk to the exit. Every step was agony. I was sure I wasn't going to make it through the rest of the day.

14

Lisa grabbed me almost the moment I took my first step off the court. "Oh, you were wonderful out there," she almost bubbled.

"Um, thanks," I responded, blinking furiously. "That was a tough match. If Evan and I had lost our doubles match . . ."

"Oh, I knew you wouldn't lose."

I pulled Lisa away from the knot of people at the exit. "I don't know. Their guys were awfully good."

"But not as good as you."

"I guess. I don't know."

Lisa glanced down at my bare legs. Just then, for the very first time, it occurred to me that I hadn't planned very well for this date. I hadn't brought anything with me, not even a pair of jeans. All I had were my sweats. Yikes. How stupid could I be?

"You're going like that?" Lisa asked playfully.

I closed my eyes briefly. "I forgot to bring a change of clothes. I usually go home like this and change. All I have are my sweats."

"Oh, that's OK," Lisa smiled. "I don't care."

I slipped free from Lisa, knelt down beside my bag, and pulled my sweats free. Fortunately, they were pretty decent sweats, ones you could be seen wearing in public. Not like some of the goofy things tennis players wear, like shocking pink and orange stripes or whatever. These were mostly black, with a racing stripe down one side.

I slipped into them quickly, and zipped up the jacket. "How's this?" I asked.

"Perfect."

I looked around for Lisa's father. But, of course, I had no idea which one of the waiting cars near the tennis courts was his.

Lisa spotted my confusion. "My dad's over there," she said quickly, pointing toward the parking lot. "He's waiting in the car."

"Which one?"

"The silver one."

"The Cadillac?" I said, trying not to stare. But the car was huge and shiny.

"Yeah, that one. Dad likes them."

"Great," I muttered. I couldn't help thinking that maybe Lisa and Evan should go out together. They were from the same world, one I wasn't even vaguely familiar with.

My legs got distinctly weaker as we made our way to the car. I wondered if I was ever going to feel at least a little normal.

The driver's-side door opened as we drew near the car. A short, burly man emerged. His hair had a touch of gray to it. He looked mean enough to bite the head off a chicken.

"Mr. James," he said gruffly. "Good to meet you. Lisa speaks quite highly of you." He made his way around the car and extended a hand. I took it, remembering to shake firmly. Still, even then, his death grip about reduced my hand to pulp.

"Glad to meet you," I squeaked.

"They won, Dad," Lisa said excitedly.

"I could see that, pumpkin," her dad growled.

"Cally's as good as I said he was, isn't he?" Lisa added.

Her dad looked at me, sizing me up. "Yes, he is. No question of that."

Lisa opened the door to the backseat and climbed in. She beckoned to me. "Come on, let's go."

I climbed in and was immediately swallowed by the backseat. It was enormous. You could have a party in the back of this car.

Lisa's dad drove us to the McDonald's in silence. He just kept his eyes on the road, while Lisa began to tell me about her day. She told me about her first period class, about the notes she'd passed to her friends. Then she told me about her second period class. She was just beginning to tell me about third period when we pulled into the parking lot.

Lisa's dad looked at his watch as we got out of the car. "About 45 minutes, honey? That be enough?"

"Yeah, Dad, that'd be great," Lisa answered.

Her dad just nodded. I didn't want to ask what he would do for those 45 minutes. Probably go out and clean some guy's clock for all I knew. Or make some deal or something.

Lisa was already into her fourth period by the time we had our food and sat down. I wondered vaguely what she'd do when she got to the end of her day. Would she talk about the day before?

I wasn't able to say much. Once Lisa got going, she could talk up a blue streak. It was all I could do to eat, mumble, and nod at the right time during the conversation.

Her hair kind of danced around while she talked too. Actually, it was interesting in its own way. When she really got animated—like when she was describing how the teacher in her fifth period intercepted one of her friend's notes and then read it out loud and how she just about *died* when he got to the part about some guy in the class—her hair flipped back and forth furiously. As a result, she was constantly pulling strands of hair out of her face.

When she finished telling me about all the notes she'd passed during her classes and what her friends were saying about everyone else in school, she answered my question. She didn't talk about the previous day's classes. She told me about her visit to the mall the night before.

She'd conned her mom into taking her. It was so cool, she said. All her other friends conned their moms into taking them. Then they met at the water fountain and they were off. They buzzed through all the stores while their moms shopped.

Lisa was describing her close call—how she almost bought a pair of shoes that didn't match one of her outfits and how she only discovered that they wouldn't match when she got home later that evening—when we climbed back into the Cadillac.

Her dad just grunted as we got in. Apparently, he already knew where we were going, because he drove us to the theater in silence. Well, not actually in silence. Lisa described her Sears experience on the way.

It was *horrible,* she said. She and her friends were wandering through the store, just for a diversion, when she actually spotted something she liked—a nice, light blue sweater with pearl buttons. But she couldn't just, like, you know, stop in the middle of Sears and buy something. Not with her friends there.

So, what she did, she whispered conspiratorially, was get her friends to go off into another store for something, and then she doubled back to buy the sweater from Sears.

"It was great," she said, beaming. "I just bought it, took it out of its bag and put it in my other bag, the one from Lord and Taylor's."

Actually, I didn't have a clue what Lord and Taylor's was. I sort of liked Sears. I could get tube socks that didn't fall down around my ankles for three bucks. And I could get pretty decent tennis shirts for six or seven bucks too.

I wasn't even looking as we finally entered the movie theater. I had just nodded when her dad said he'd pick us up in front in a couple of hours.

"Hi, Cally," Elaine said, not more than three feet from me as we walked into the lobby.

I looked up, startled. Elaine Cimons was standing right in front of me. She was standing with Jason Pittman, who looked distinctly uncomfortable. His wire-rimmed glasses were even kind of steamed up. And one of his nicely creased pants legs was just a little crumpled. He looked different, away from our Bible study.

I stood there in shock for a moment, staring at Elaine. It was almost as if she'd been there ahead of me, waiting. But, of course, that was crazy. She didn't know I was going to a movie with Lisa. How could she have known that, anyway?

"Oh, hi, Elaine," I said finally.

Lisa and Elaine just glared at each other for a second, and then said "hi" to each other. I just nodded at Jason.

"You're seeing this movie?" I asked Elaine moronically.

"No, I thought I'd just stand here in the lobby with Jason," Elaine said sarcastically. "Of course I'm seeing the movie. Jason and I have talked about seeing it for a while."

Jason turned to Elaine with a puzzled look on his face. "Actually, you just mentioned it to me . . ."

Elaine stumbled and stepped on Jason's foot. Almost like it was on purpose. "Oh, I'm really sorry, Jason," Elaine said, catching Jason before he tumbled to the ground. "Did I hurt you?"

"No," Jason said, straightening his glasses. "But I was just saying . . ."

"Hey, we'd better get going," Elaine said quickly, cutting Jason off. "We don't want to miss the movie."

"No, we don't," Lisa said, almost as quickly. "Why don't you two go on? We still have to buy some popcorn. Maybe we'll see you after the movie or something."

"Maybe," Elaine said, glancing back and forth between Lisa and me. Then she turned and left, dragging Jason with her.

"Well?" Lisa asked me.

"Well, what?" I responded, about as thoroughly confused as I'd ever been.

"Are you going to buy me some popcorn, or do I have to buy it myself?"

"Oh, yeah, um, sure. I'll go stand in line."

Lisa nodded. "Great. That'll give me a chance to go to the little girls' room. I'll be right back. Promise."

As I stood waiting in line to get popcorn, I started to think about how curious it was that I'd run into Elaine. Here, of all places, and with Jason Pittman. Jason Pittman? It made no sense.

When I got to the counter, I decided to buy two boxes of Milk Duds. I didn't really like popcorn. Actually, I sort of hated popcorn. It got stuck in your teeth, and it always made you incredibly thirsty. So I figured I could sort of slip Milk Duds in my mouth and chew quietly during the movie.

Lisa was gone at least five minutes. I waited and watched the clock. The movie had already started by the time we got to the theater. Lisa looked over the darkened theater until she'd seen what she was looking for—Elaine and Jason sitting a third of the way up on the right. Lisa headed over to the back and the far left of the theater.

The seats were way back, exactly where I hate it. I like to sit up near the front. And not surprisingly, Lisa talked throughout the whole movie. I didn't hear half of the movie. She commented on almost everything that happened.

I was delighted when it was over. I'd polished off both boxes of Milk Duds, and I was thoroughly sick to my stomach.

When Lisa's dad pulled up in front of the "barn" and let me out, Lisa reached over and gave me a quick peck on the cheek.

"I had a great time, Cally!" she bubbled. "Thanks for asking me. Really. This was fabulous."

"Yeah, cool," I muttered, trying to back away from the car and the open door without falling into the ditch at the side of the driveway.

"See you at school on Monday," she said, waving. "We'll talk." She slammed the door, and the car roared off an instant later.

As I walked slowly up the driveway to the house, it occurred to me that at least one good thing had happened that evening. My legs were no longer wobbly, my heart no longer pounded, and my hands were no longer clammy. I was definitely no longer nervous.

But my brain was mush. My ears were about talked off. And I still couldn't remember how that dumb movie had ended. Lisa had been talking during the final scene, and I'd missed the last part. Oh, well.

Elaine had bumped into us again as we were leaving. But she hadn't said a word to me. There was just this look of absolute fury on her face as she and Jason had left the theater. I wondered if maybe there had been something in the movie she didn't like.

Jana and Karen were there waiting for me as I came in.

"So?" Jana asked, all ears.

"I'll tell you later," I mumbled and started to head upstairs to my room.

"Did you see Elaine?" Karen asked.

I stopped and stared at my sister. "Elaine? How'd you know she'd be there?"

Karen just smiled. "Oh, I talked to her last night. She called. We were just talking. I told her what you were doing tonight, and where you were going. She said she just happened to be doing the very same thing. Going to that same movie, I mean."

I couldn't believe what I was hearing. Karen and Elaine talked? I just grunted and continued my trek up the stairs. I decided on the way up that there were just some things I'd never quite get. Not in a million years.

Mom decided that the whole crew couldn't go see John's spelling bee. She was afraid that if John didn't do well, it would be too hard having the entire family there.

So, instead, Mom took a leave of absence from work on Tuesday and picked me up from school after my second period. Mom had sent a note to my principal, who'd agreed to let me out of school for the bee.

The spelling bee at Thompson was quite an event. All six grades got to come to the auditorium for the event, during the middle of the day.

This was actually the second time one of the James kids had been in a spelling bee. Karen had won her class spelling bee when she was in the fifth grade, but she'd been knocked out in the second round of her school's championship on "frankincense." She'd spelled it with an "s" instead of a "c."

The auditorium was jam-packed with loud, squirming kids by the time Mom and I arrived. Most of the kids in the bee were already up on stage. John was nowhere to be seen, though. Mom looked around the auditorium frantically, trying to spot him.

"That'd be just like him," I mumbled under my breath. "Miss the dumb thing."

"Cally!" Mom whispered sharply. "He won't miss this."

We were standing just inside the double doors at the back of the auditorium where most of the kids usually entered. I didn't even hear Dr. Burnley slip up behind me.

"Hello, Mrs. James, Cally," she said softly. "If you're looking for John, I saw him with one of his friends just a little while ago. His friend was crying, and John was sitting with him."

"Crying?" Mom asked.

"Not John," Dr. Burnley said. "One of his friends."

John had only a couple of friends that I knew of—the twins, Mickey and Mark. So it had to be one of them. Then I remembered what John had been talking about the other day, about one of them being sick or something.

"Was it Mickey or Mark?" I asked.

Dr. Burnley nodded. "Yes, it was one of the Landis twins. Mickey, I think. I'm not sure what the problem is, though."

"I think I know," I said softly.

Mom gave me a quizzical look. She didn't have a clue what was going on here. "What . . . ?" she began to ask.

"I'll tell you later," I said with a frown. "I think Mark's sick."

"Sick?"

I could see Dr. Burnley nodding her head. "He's been out of school for a week or so now. I do remember that, now."

Mom looked back and forth between Dr. Burnley and me, probably wondering how it was that she didn't know something that so obviously involved John and how we did.

But just at that moment, I saw John walk onto the stage from the back. He sort of slipped from behind one of the heavy drapes and took a chair on stage.

I pointed at the stage. Mom looked over, then. A big wave of relief went across her face. She stared patiently at the stage until John saw the two of us standing at the back of the auditorium. Mom waved. So did I. John just adjusted his glasses and nodded back at us.

The auditorium grew silent finally as the principal walked onto the stage and explained the rules. He asked the other kids in the audience to be quiet during the contest, so the kids on stage could hear the words. Miraculously, they were quiet.

I wondered how many in the auditorium knew that John wasn't a fifth- or sixth-grader. Not many of them, I'd guess. And those who knew most likely didn't care too much one way or another.

Everyone on stage made it through the first two rounds easily. The words they asked were easy, like "gourd" and "primary" and "spindle."

But in the third round, they started asking tougher words. Three kids dropped out by the time they got to John. I was fidgeting as John eased out of his chair and walked to the microphone at the front of the stage.

At least some of the kids had already dropped out, I thought. So if he doesn't make it here, he won't be the first to go.

"The word is 'epoxy,'" one of the judges read.

I looked at John. He just nodded, thought for a moment, and then spelled it correctly, with an "e" at the front and not an "a" or something goofy. If I hadn't drilled John on that word, I might have gotten it wrong myself.

John took his seat when the judge told him he had spelled it correctly. I tried to catch his eye, to give him a "thumbs up" signal, but John wouldn't have anything to do with it. He was totally focused on the contest, and he wasn't about to let anything distract him.

Good for him, I thought. I was just like this during a tennis match. I tried not to see anyone in the stands during important matches—not my friends, my family, anyone. I just kept my eye on the ball at all times.

Four more kids were gone by the time John's turn came up again. I held my breath again. But I could see that John was gaining a little confidence, now. He walked right up to the mike without any hesitation.

His word this time was "integer." I was pretty sure I knew how it was spelled. I wasn't altogether sure I knew what it meant, however. Something to do with math. Whole numbers, or something like that.

Again, John didn't ask the judges to use it in a sentence or anything like that, like nearly all of the other kids were doing by now. He just listened closely as the judge pronounced the word, then he spelled it correctly.

The audience cheered just a little louder for John. I was sure of it. So maybe some of them did know that John was just a fourth-grader. It was mostly the younger kids who were cheering for him.

There were only five kids left when John's turn came up again. All five were kids who had not hesitated over a single word. I figured John would now lose to one of these kids.

But he had done tremendously well, I reasoned. Everything would be just fine. He had not failed miserably. He had nearly won the contest. It would be OK if he dropped out now.

But John didn't drop out. Neither did any of the other kids. It was clear to me that they'd all studied that little book with all the words, just like John had.

When it became clear that the five on stage weren't about to miss one of the words from that book, the judges conferred for a few seconds and then announced that they would go to the additional book of words, which was much, much harder.

There was no way you could memorize every single word in this larger book. Not even John, I didn't imagine. John and I had drilled from it, and he hadn't gotten anything wrong. But I just didn't think he could remember every word from it.

Two kids dropped out in the first round from this larger book of words. The words were much harder. I mean, they had words like "inspissate" in this bunch. Who in the world had ever heard of such a word, much less used it?

I felt sorry for the kid who got that word. Hearing it used in a sentence—something about inspissating the chicken broth—did nothing for the poor kid. He got the second "s" right. It was the "i" in the middle he missed.

John was last to go in this round. "The word is 'peroneal,'" the judge said.

For the first time, John asked him to please repeat the word and use it in a sentence. I couldn't tell whether it was because John was stalling, or if he just wanted to make sure it was the same word he was thinking of.

My heart had long ago stopped beating. I'd never heard of the stupid word. I didn't have a clue what it was, much less how to spell it. I figured the first part could be "e," "a," or even "ea." I figured the second syllable could be either "o" or "a." I hadn't even gotten to the third syllable.

"The peroneal is located near the outer portion of the leg," the judge said.

John nodded once and then spelled the word. Correctly. With an "e" and an "o" and an "ea."

The whole place cheered wildly when the judge said "correct" and John turned to sit down in his seat. They were all rooting for him now. I could see it. So could Mom.

Mom had been deathly silent up to this point, her hands clenched tightly at her side. But now she let out a cheer along with the other kids when John got the word right.

One of the three remaining kids missed a word before it came around to John again. There were now just two remaining—John and a girl who looked a great deal older and smarter than John, by a long shot. She was clearly a sixth-grader, and she had clearly studied quite hard for this contest. She hadn't hesitated yet over a single word.

John got another word I'd never heard of "chiasmus." But I could at least figure out how to spell it in my mind. It had three syllables, and they were probably just as they sounded.

John asked the judge to use it in a sentence. A "chiasmus" was, it turned out, something to do with rhetorical speech. *Great,* I thought glumly. *That helps a lot.*

But John got it right. The whole place shook from the cheers. The other girl on the stage just stared straight ahead, every bit as determined as John.

They went through a second round like that. Then a third, a fourth, and a fifth. I recognized about half the words the judges were throwing at them. But they were both knocking them down right and left.

John was absolutely marvelous. But so was the girl beside him. She spelled each word quickly, crisply, without hesitation.

John hesitated briefly on what I thought was a simple word, "prolate." He asked the judge to repeat it. John wanted to know if it was "prelate" or "prolate."

The judge merely shook his head, indicating he could only repeat the word and use it in a sentence, something about a "prolate spheroid." *That helped,* I thought miserably.

I could see the wheels spinning in John's head. He wasn't altogether sure which word it was, whether he'd heard it right or not. But he spelled it with an "o," the judge told him he'd gotten it right, and John breathed a big sigh of relief. So did Mom and I.

John's competitor grimaced. I could see that she was hoping John would miss soon. I noticed that she was crossing her fingers every time John stepped up to the microphone. John, on the other hand, usually looked around when it was her turn.

They went through three more rounds, each getting their words right, the girl never stumbling or hesitating.

And then she got a "q" word, a "quincunx." It was something to do with five objects laid out in a rectangle, with something in the middle. I'd never heard of the word. It was clear the girl hadn't either.

She asked the judge to repeat it. Then she asked him to use it in a sentence. Then she asked him to repeat it again.

The girl looked down at her shoes, over at the judges, down at her shoes again, and then over her shoulder at John to see if he knew the word. But John wasn't looking either at her or the judges. He was studying something off to the side of the stage.

She spelled the first three letters quickly. She thought a long time before saying "k" for the fourth letter and then adding "u," "n," and "x."

"I'm sorry, that's wrong," the judge said with a somber voice. A hush fell over the crowd. John eased his way out of his chair and walked up to the microphone. If he got this word right and then spelled his own word correctly, he won.

John didn't even hesitate for a moment. He spelled it exactly as the girl had — except that he substituted a "c" where she had said "k."

"Correct," the judge said. The auditorium erupted, and then calmed down again as the judge read John his final word. It was "ecesis" and, again, I'd never heard of it. It had something to do with an organism surviving in a brand-new environment. Sort of like what John was trying to do.

John smiled just a little, and then spelled it correctly. Mom gave me a huge hug as the place cheered and cheered. I couldn't believe it. John had won. He had actually won. He was going on to the state championship.

It was weird. Mom and I waited for John after the spelling bee. We were going to take him out for ice cream to celebrate, and the very first thing John said had absolutely nothing whatsoever to do with the spelling bee.

He wanted to know if he could ask Mickey over to spend the night. On a school night, no less.

"But why, honey?" Mom asked gently. We were standing just outside the back entrance to the auditorium. The other kids had mostly gone back to their classes, after pounding and pummeling John's back to congratulate him.

John's face was flushed from all the excitement of winning. But I could see that he was much more interested in getting Mom to agree to let his friend come over for the night.

"Just because," John said. "Can I do that instead of going out for ice cream right now? Can I?"

Mom looked over at me to see if I had a clue what was going on. I shook my head. This was all new to me.

"John, can you at least tell me why you'd like to invite your friend over tonight?" she asked him.

John fixed his very best stare on Mom. "'Cause I want to ask him about Mark," he said firmly. "I want to know everything about it. Maybe I can figure out why Mark is sick."

"Mark is sick?"

"They took him to the hospital on Sunday," John said quickly. "He's really sick, Mom. He sleeps almost all the time now, Mickey says. He's so tired he can't get up and do anything, so they took him to the hospital."

Mom smiled wanly. "John, I think it would be wonderful if you had your friend, Mickey, over for the night if his parents will let him. But I think we should let the doctors try to understand what's wrong with Mark. That's what they're trained to do."

John pursed his lips angrily. "But, Mom! They don't know what's wrong with him. Mickey says they've done all these tests, and they can't figure it out."

"And you think you can help?" Mom asked, amused.

"I know I can," John nodded. "I thought maybe I'd read through a bunch of stuff, after Mickey tells me about what's wrong with Mark. And then maybe I could find something."

Mom nodded. "Well, I'll tell you what. I'll give Mrs. Landis a call this afternoon, see if Mickey wants to spend the night and if it's all right. But if his mom says he can't, no complaining. Promise?"

John nodded. "I promise. But try hard, OK?"

"I will," Mom said solemnly, and then took John's hand fondly. "It's nice of you to think of your friend, though. Especially after you've just won such an important contest."

John frowned. "Ah, it isn't so important. I just hope I can help Mark. I know I can. I'll read and read and read until I find something. You just watch."

Mom laughed. It was good to see John so energized. "Maybe you're right, John. But you know we'll have to go to the state championship, in Richmond, in three days. It's this Friday evening."

"I'll study up for that, I promise," John vowed. "If Cally will help."

I nodded. "I'll help. Don't you worry about that, kid. We're gonna start on the dictionary now."

17

So, instead of ice cream, John celebrated his victory with a friend. When Mom talked to Mrs. Landis, she was more than delighted to see her son's attention diverted.

Because, it turned out, Mom told me later, Mark was very, very sick. The doctors were convinced it was leukemia, just as I'd guessed.

But what they couldn't figure out was how he'd gotten so sick so fast. Or why the tests wouldn't confirm that he actually had leukemia.

Mom said Mrs. Landis started crying while they were talking. She was afraid Mark would die soon, and they still weren't even entirely sure what was wrong.

John started bugging me right away, from the moment I arrived home after school. He cornered me in the kitchen before dinner, while I was trying to steal a few cookies. Mickey was up in his room, working on a new model airplane kit Mom had bought especially for tonight.

But what John wanted to know about was how he could read about medical things. Right up my alley.

"Why're you asking me?" I complained.

"Because you're supposed to know things like that," John answered.

"Yeah, says who?"

"Who else can I ask?" John persisted.

"Ask Mom."

"I did. She doesn't know how."

"If she doesn't know how, then why in the world do you think I can help?" I snapped.

John just looked at me placidly, undisturbed by my outburst. "You always figure things out, that's why."

"But not this!"

"Just try, OK, Cally?"

OK, I thought glumly. John wanted to read medical literature, about sicknesses and disease and stuff like that. Great. I didn't know where you went to find that. Did you go up to the librarian at school and say, excuse me, please, can you tell me how to learn what doctors learn at medical school?

Of course not. But a glimmer of an idea had occurred to me. There was one person I knew, someone who'd already bailed me out once, who might be able to help. But, in the meantime, I needed to see what I was up against.

"Let's go upstairs," I said quietly. "I need to talk to Mickey."

"OK," John agreed, and turned to leave the kitchen.

"Just how sick is Mark, anyway?" I asked John as we trudged up the stairs to John's room.

"Pretty sick. Mickey said he hardly woke up today at all, only for a few minutes."

I didn't say anything until we'd gotten to the top of the stairs. "Do they still think it's leukemia?"

John shook his head. "No, they did the blood tests, Mickey says, and now they're pretty sure it isn't leukemia."

"Then what . . . ?"

"They don't know," John whispered. "But whatever it is, it's really bad."

We walked into John's room. Mickey was perched on one corner of John's bed, which was neat as a pin except for the model airplane kit strewn across every inch of his bed.

Mickey was small for his age, probably three inches smaller than John. He had strawberry blond hair, and he was wiry. Mark looked exactly like him, of course. They even wore the same clothes most of the time.

"What's that smell?" I asked, crinkling up my nose.

"It's the new airplane glue Mom got me," John answered.

Mickey looked up then. "Yeah, we ran out of the glue at our house that we'd been using. So your mom got some new glue at the store today. It works great. Our glue was pretty old, and it didn't always hold like this glue does."

"I see," I mumbled. I didn't know good airplane glue from rotten airplane glue. Glue was glue.

"It's gonna be an old B-52," Mickey said proudly.

"That's great," I said. I settled down on another corner of the bed. I watched the two of them work at their task for a while.

They worked well together. John figured out what went where. Mickey found the part, painstakingly applied the glue, and affixed it to the growing airplane.

I noticed how careful Mickey was. He had the kind of patience with small parts that I never had. I was a major league klutz with small things in my hands. Give me a big, old tennis racquet any day, something I could hold onto.

"Oh, crud!" Mickey said at one point.

John started laughing. "Just eat it the way Mark does."

I looked over at Mickey. Some of the glue had squished out the side of one of the parts. No big deal, as far as I was concerned. But it was a trauma to the makers of the plane.

"No way," Mickey said, turning up his nose. "He likes the taste of glue. Not me."

I gave the two of them a strange look. "You mean Mark eats the airplane glue?"

Mickey rolled his eyes. "Yeah, he's always doing junk like that. He says the glue tastes good."

"Yuck," I grimaced.

John got up from the bed. "I'll go get a washcloth. Hang on."

"Okay, I'll wait. Hurry," Mickey said.

While John was gone, I took the opportunity to ask Mickey a couple of things. But I was careful. "Did you see Mark at the hospital today?" I asked.

Mickey nodded. "Yeah, but he was mostly asleep. They tried to give him his dinner, but he wouldn't eat it again. So he had the tube stuff."

"The tube stuff?"

"You know," Mickey frowned, "they hook him up to those tubes and feed him that way."

I nodded, understanding. They were feeding Mark intravenously. He really was in bad shape, if he couldn't eat for himself and he slept all the time. "Were you able to talk to him?"

"Not much. I brought him a new airplane. But it's just sitting beside his bed."

Mickey was looking down at the bed, now. I figured I'd better not press it much further. "Do they know what the problem is yet, so they can try to help him get better?"

Mickey didn't look up. "Mom says it isn't what they thought before, that it's not leukemia. Now the doctors are saying that it's . . . it's, um, what's the word for when you're really tired all the time?"

I thought for a moment. "Anemia?"

Mickey nodded vigorously. "Yeah, that's it. They said it's some kind of anemia. They said he doesn't have enough of this certain kind of white blood cell, a granu something or other."

"Hmm," I mumbled. "But they still don't know exactly what the problem is?"

"Nope. He's just dizzy and weak a lot. He throws up sometimes, though not as much now that he isn't eating anymore."

John came back in the room, then, carrying a wet washcloth. He tossed it at Mickey. The washcloth hit him in the chest and fell into his lap.

"I hope that isn't one of Mom's good washcloths," I warned.

"Don't worry," John said. "It isn't."

I got up to leave. I'd heard enough. I don't know what I was looking for, exactly. Maybe just enough to know what I was talking about when I went to see my new friend about finding reading material for John.

"Hey, I'll see you guys," I said as I made my way to the door.

"Tell Mom to call us for dinner?" John asked.

"Sure. No problem," I answered, closing the door behind me. They were already hard at work. Mickey had cleaned the glue from the airplane, carefully wiping it away without disturbing the body of the airplane.

As I walked back down the stairs to the kitchen, a deep despair began to settle on me. It really made no sense at all. Mark and Mickey were identical twins. Why would one get so sick and the other remain healthy? How was that possible?

Oh well, I thought. That's what they pay doctors a billion dollars for, to figure stuff like that out.

The phone rang. Jana sprinted across the living room to get to the phone first. I don't know why she hurried. No one challenged her. "Hello," she answered breathlessly. After a couple of seconds, a smirk spread across her face.

"It's your girlfriend," she whispered, holding the phone out toward me.

"Lisa is not my girlfriend," I protested.

Jana just laughed. "Yeah, sure. Whatever."

The despair settling even more around me, I took the phone and sat down in the chair near the phone. I braced myself. I'd have to hear about her day again, probably starting with what she had for breakfast.

"Hey, Cally," Lisa said excitedly. "You know what happened to me in first period today . . . ?"

At least this time I knew right where to go. And, luckily, Dr. Burnley was in her office when I arrived before school started the next day.

She rose from behind her desk and came around to extend a hand. "Well, Cally, this is a pleasant surprise. What can I do for you?"

I immediately began to fidget. I finally decided to just get right to the point. "I wanted to ask for your help again."

"Shoot."

"John wants to read through a bunch of medical stuff, to see if he can find something that might help his friend."

"Medical stuff?"

"You know, books and literature. That kind of thing."

Dr. Burnley nodded. "Oh, I see. Like *The Merck Manual*. That kind of literature?"

I looked at Dr. Burnley helplessly. I'd never heard of that manual before. I didn't even know where to begin. "Something that tells you about what's wrong with people."

A worried look crossed Dr. Burnley's face. "Is something wrong in your family?"

"No, it's one of John's friends," I said quickly. "He's got this kind of anemia, but I guess it's really serious. They think he'll die soon."

"I see," Dr. Burnley nodded. She turned to look at her bookshelves. She pulled a book down and kept looking. She pulled another book down, and then two more. She turned and handed them to me. "John can look up the anemias in the indexes at the back."

"Is it all right to just borrow these?" I asked.

"Sure," she laughed. "Just return them when you're finished. They're my old college textbooks."

"Will he understand them?" I asked.

"Probably not. But that hardly matters. Just looking will do John a world of good."

I tucked the books under my arm. "You know, I never did say thank you . . ."

Dr. Burnley cut me off quickly. "No need to, Cally. Like I said, I get paid to do this."

"I know, but . . ."

"I was delighted to see how well John did at the spelling bee," she said firmly. "I think it surprised a lot of people around here."

A thought occurred to me. "You know, now that he's won the spelling bee, maybe people can see he's not dumb after all and that maybe he shouldn't be in that special class."

Dr. Burnley smiled ever so slightly. "It doesn't quite work that way, Cally. Your brother still has some problems, some hurdles to overcome. He'll get there. I have confidence in him. In you."

"In me?"

"Yes, you. He looks up to you in a very big way, in case you hadn't noticed."

"I guess," I shrugged. "But you're sure he can't duck out of that special class?"

"I'm sure, Cally," Dr. Burnley said, a funny look in her eyes. "You'll just have to trust me on this. I know what I'm talking about."

I really didn't want to leave it at that. But what choice did I have? "OK, well, anyway, thanks for the books. I'll bring them back as soon as John's finished with them."

"No hurry."

I turned to leave, but not before I gave it one more shot. "You know, not everyone can win a spelling bee the way John did. You have to be pretty smart to do that."

"No one ever said John was stupid, Cally. That isn't the problem here."

"But, I mean, he won the spelling bee!"

"It's the other parts of his life, of his mind, that need help," Dr. Burnley said softly. "Beyond his rote memory. Cally, keep working at it. You'll see."

I clenched my fists. I *didn't* see. John had won the spelling bee. I knew *I* couldn't have done that—no one in our family except John could have done that. Yet they still wanted to hold him back. It made no sense at all. None.

"All right," I grumbled. "I'll keep thinking about it. But I just know John isn't stupid. He isn't."

"I know, Cally. He isn't. You're right. But he does need help."

My shoulders slumped. I knew when I was defeated. "OK, well, I'll see you, then. I'll be late to school."

"Let me know what John finds in those books, OK?" she called out after me. "I'd like to know."

John devoured the books. He absolutely consumed them. I'd never seen him like this. He had all four books spread out on his bed. He just kept going back and forth between them, comparing pages and words and phrases.

I was sure he didn't understand half the language used in the manuals, stuff about idiopathic cases and aplastic bone marrow and hemolytic anemias.

John didn't seem to mind at all, though. It was probably just like everything else to him. He understood some things and not others. This was no different. He understood some of the words and not the others. He understood some of the language and not the rest.

He was looking for clues, some thread between all the different descriptions of acute anemia and the twins. He had no idea what he was looking for. I had no idea what he was looking for.

But it didn't matter. John was consumed. On Thursday, he brought home more books from the school's library, more general medical books on different things. He spread all of those out on his bed too.

I don't know how he managed it, but Mickey's mom even gave him a readout of the lab tests from one of Mark's doctors. It had some of the results of the lab test and everything. John showed it to me proudly.

"See the lab results?" he asked me, pointing to a place on the Xeroxed piece of paper. "It says his granulocyte count is way below 1,500 and that his serum iron is too high."

I gave John a strange look. "You know what a granulocyte is?"

"Yeah, sure," John answered. "It's a white blood cell."

I just nodded and listened as John continued. "And see here? His platelets are way down. But the color of his blood is normal. That's why they thought it might be leukemia."

I looked at John again. "And you know what serum iron and platelets are?"

John shook his head. "Um, not really. But, see, what I'm doing, I'm learning everything I can about Mark and then I'm looking for the same things in everything I'm reading."

"So every time you see those same words, you compare them?"

"Yeah, exactly."

"I get it," I nodded. It actually made sense. Sort of. I wasn't sure it would ever lead to anything. But it sure didn't hurt anything.

"You *are* going to have time to study your words with me, right?" I asked him.

"Sure, yeah, tonight. Is that okay?"

"Will that give us enough time?"

John nodded. "You know I've already read through all the spelling books, don't you?"

"I know. I just thought maybe we could study the dictionary."

John didn't say anything right away. "I guess I should have told you this, but I did that awhile ago. I kind of went through every page."

"Of the dictionary?" I asked, incredulous.

"Yeah, I figured it might help. If I looked at every word, I thought that, maybe, somehow, it might help me understand things better."

I was shocked. He'd actually looked through the dictionary. "So did it help?"

John smiled. It was nice to see it on him. "Nope. It didn't. But I sure do know how to spell a lot of words now."

----20

John really was prepared for the state championship in Richmond that Friday evening. More prepared than I could have imagined. It was almost as if he'd been practicing his whole life for this.

He really *had* gone through the dictionary. And what amazed me, which was hard with John these days, was that he remembered words he'd looked at in the dictionary.

This time, the whole family went—all except Timmy, who stayed with Aunt Franny. He was still just a little too young to sit still in an auditorium for a few hours. Mom took a couple hours of leave from work, and we all left after school let out.

John took a whole bunch of his medical books with him. That's what he studied during the 90-minute drive from Washington to Richmond. Not his spelling words.

Mom told me not to say anything, just to leave it alone. Maybe it was John's way of relaxing before the contest, she warned me. It wasn't as if John could actually learn more words right before the contest anyway.

It made some sense. But I was also quite sure something had happened to John, something wonderful and miraculous, something that would carry forward with him the rest of his life.

John had found a purpose for the strange working of his brain. He'd found a way to gather up all the bits and pieces of information that constantly floated around inside his mind and try to make some sense out of all of it.

It was quite interesting to watch him at work. He'd mumble about some phrase he'd come across in one book and then he'd double-check it against a phrase he remembered from somewhere else.

Toward the end of the trip, John looked up with a flushed, feverish look on his face. He was sitting in the front seat by himself, next to Mom, who was driving. The rest of us were crammed in the back of the car.

John turned and looked at me over the back of the seat. There was a wild excitement in his eyes, one I'd never seen in John before. He'd found something. I was certain of it. John had found something.

"What is it?" I asked him.

"I think I know," John almost whispered.

"What?" I asked again. "What did you find?"

All the other kids in the car stopped chattering for just a second. Every eye, every ear, was now trained on John. Even Susan was quiet. Chris stopped harassing his two older sisters.

John could hardly talk he was so excited. "I think . . . I think it's the airplane glue," he said at last.

"The airplane glue?" I said, dumbfounded.

"The airplane glue," John repeated.

"Where in the world . . . ?" I asked.

John just smiled. It was a contented smile, one that came from knowing that he'd finally stumbled across something.

"You see," John began, "it all makes sense now. Once I knew that it was aplastic anemia and that it was his bone marrow that wasn't working, I started reading just the stuff about that. That's all I looked at, in every section."

Mom glanced over at John briefly, though she quickly turned her gaze back to the highway. "John, do you know what aplastic anemia is?"

John shook his head. "No. I mean, I've read about it and all. But I don't exactly know what it is."

"Then how do you know it's the airplane glue?" I asked.

John started nodding vigorously. "Because I started reading about all this stuff that causes aplastic anemia. There's all sorts of junk that does that."

"Like?"

"Things like arsenic, radiation, and benzene," John answered. "Other stuff too. Then I started reading about where all this stuff comes from and how it can get in people. And that's when I finally found it. And now it all makes sense."

"What exactly did you find, John?" Mom asked gently.

John shifted in his seat. His hands were folded under his legs. He was all hunched up in the seat. "Airplane glue sometimes has benzene in it. That's what one of the books said. And Mark always eats the airplane glue. Mickey doesn't . . ."

"That's right," I said, remembering the discussion from John's bedroom.

"Mark *eats* the airplane glue?" Jana asked from way back in the car. "Yuck!"

"Yeah, that's gross!" Chris seconded.

"Hush!" Mom said sharply. "Let John finish." The car grew silent again, except for the steady drone from the tires rolling over the pavement.

"Anyway," John began again, "like I said, I started looking for things that all this stuff was in, and that's when I found out about the airplane glue. It was in this book." John held up a thick tome of some kind.

"Let me see," I demanded.

John handed the book to me over the seat. He pointed out the passage. Sure enough, there it was, in black and white—one sentence buried in the middle of a very long, complicated, tongue-twisting passage about benzene and toxic agents. It talked about exposure to benzene in model airplane glue.

"When I saw that, I remembered about Mark. It all made sense. The benzene got into Mark. That's what's causing it. Another book I read said benzene messes up your bone marrow, which is Mark's problem."

"So what now?" I asked.

John shrugged. "I don't know. Another book I read said that if you keep any more of the poison from getting in him . . ."

"What?" I asked.

"The benzene," John said. "If you do that, then Mark can get better."

"And if he doesn't get better?"

John thought for a brief moment. "Another book I looked at said something about bone marrow transplants in identical twins. That works sometimes."

I shook my head in awe. I had no idea if John was right, if he'd actually found something. But that still, small voice that somehow makes its presence known in my life told me that John had, indeed, found something.

21

There were probably hundreds of kids on the stage at the civic center in downtown Richmond. John was swallowed up in the middle of that sea of smart kids.

But it didn't take long for the group to shrink. The judges didn't even bother with the easier words. They started right off with the hardest words from the extra word books. About half dropped out in the first round alone.

The center was jammed with parents, brothers, sisters, aunts, uncles, grandmothers, and grandfathers. There were easily five people for every one contestant. Our family was just one of many in the throng.

We arrived too late to find good seats up near the front, so Mom decided to keep us all together, and we took a row of seats toward the back of the auditorium.

John gave us one small wave and a "thumbs up" sign right before the competition started. Then he ignored us, just like I'd instructed him. Keep your eye on the judges and the words, not the crowd, I'd told him.

John breezed through the first five rounds. He didn't even ask the judges how the word was used in those rounds, unlike nearly every other kid on the stage.

By then, there were only six kids left. John was by far the smallest of the six. He looked even smaller when he sat on his hands and scrunched into his seat.

The contest shifted into high gear then. The judges pulled out the big book of words compiled from the general dictionary, announced to the crowd that any word was fair game, and plunged in.

Three more kids fell out under this new round. I didn't recognize a single word in this bunch.

John's word was "officinal." John asked for its usage. "The doctor gave the patient an 'officinal' drug, so a prescription was not required," the judge responded.

Yikes, I thought. *Where did they get these words anyway?*

John hesitated only briefly and then spelled it correctly. There was sporadic cheering. No one here knew who John was. He was just some kid with a name tag that said "Thompson Elementary School, Northern Virginia" on the front of his shirt.

It took another two rounds for one of the remaining three to drop out, on a word I was *quite* sure had never been used in any, single conversation in America until this very moment.

And then it was down to John and another boy, nearly as small and reserved as John. The two of them traded four more words. The whole place got very still, all things considered. Most of the people had stayed to see the end of the contest, even though their own child or relative had long ago dropped out.

I figured it was only a matter of time before they came across a word John hadn't seen before, and that would be that. I had no idea if John could spell a word correctly he'd never seen.

But it was the other boy who came across that word first. The whole place could see it from the moment the judge read the word. The boy, so small in the middle of the big stage, almost disappeared when the word was read. His head dropped to his chest almost immediately. It didn't come up right away, but when it did we could all see that he didn't know the word.

He gave it a valiant try. He had the judge use it in a sentence, stalled, asked the judge to repeat it and then spelled it very slowly and deliberately.

I looked at John while the boy was spelling the word. John, as usual, was looking elsewhere. For all I knew, he was thinking about model airplane glue and benzene. *Well, good for him,* I thought. *That's what matters anyway, isn't it?*

"I'm sorry, that is incorrect," one of the judges said. About half of the crowd groaned.

John stepped up to the microphone, his hands buried in his pockets. He didn't pause, even for a moment. He spelled the word quickly and then waited.

"Correct," the judge said. The other half of the crowd now pulling for him erupted in a cheer and then grew silent again as the judges conferred over the word that could determine the state championship.

"The word is 'eudemon,'" one of the judges said. I almost started laughing, hearing the judge say it.

It reminded me of what loud, drunk people yell at contestants sometimes during a sports match. "YOU DE MAN!" they'll yell loudly. That's what this word sounded like.

John asked the judge to use it in a sentence. "The people were not fearful of the eudemon," the judge answered.

No help there, I thought. I looked over at Mom. Her face was white as a sheet. Everyone else in our family was leaning forward on the edge of their seats, wishing and hoping.

John answered a moment later. "E−u−d−e−m−o−n," he said.

The crowd held its breath. "Correct," the judge said, and the auditorium shook from the cheers.

The reporters in the state capital surged forward. The photographers snapped their pictures. Within moments, they'd surrounded him, peppering him with questions.

We made our way up to the stage as quickly as we could. But we couldn't get to him through the sea of reporters right away, not until Mom just barged through.

Mom and John hugged, ignoring the swarm of press around them and all the other well-wishers who stopped to congratulate him.

I stood on the fringe, wondering if this was the end of the road for John, or if there was still more to come. Somehow, I knew instinctively that John had only begun. The national spelling bee championship was just a week away.

The pictures in all the newspapers the next day were of John hugging Mom. I had to admit, it was a great picture—John's glasses slightly askew, tears streaming down Mom's face.

John was still the same old John, though. With one exception. He didn't talk about the spelling bee or the national championship or the newspapers or anything like that. There was only one thing he cared about. It was the only thing we talked about on the drive home from Richmond.

John had wanted to go by the Landis' house as soon as we got home that evening after the spelling bee. But it was nearly 10 P.M. when we pulled into the driveway, and Mom wasn't about to go knocking on someone's door at that hour.

So Mom, John, and I piled back into the car the next morning, while all the other kids were either asleep or watching the Saturday morning cartoons.

John was so excited, he wouldn't even look at *The Washington Post* or the other two local newspapers. Never mind that John's face and name were plastered all over the front page. He had just one thing on his mind.

"Come on, Mom," he'd pleaded. "I don't need breakfast. I'll eat later. Let's just go over to Mickey's house right now."

"John, John, calm down," Mom had said soothingly. "It's still the crack of dawn. The sun is barely up."

"Oh, the sun's been up for hours," John had scoffed.

In the end, Mom relented. She called over to Mrs. Landis to make sure they were up and that it was all right to pay a visit. She didn't even attempt to explain the nature of the visit. Mrs. Landis didn't ask.

"Boy, if it says there's benzene in that airplane glue," John mused as we drove to the house.

A thought occurred to me. "You know, didn't you say that Mickey had run out of glue? Which is why Mom had to buy the new airplane glue when Mickey came over recently."

John looked up, a pained expression on his face. "I never thought of that," he said in a small voice.

"Ah, I'll bet we can find an empty tube," I said reassuringly. "Or we can go to the store to find another tube. Don't worry."

John just grimaced. "It's an old kind. They don't make that kind of glue anymore."

"Don't worry, John," Mom tried. "It'll all work out."

But John was silent the rest of the trip to the Landis' house. He only spoke once. "I *know* I remember seeing benzene on the label of one of those tubes," he muttered.

"We believe you, dear," Mom had answered.

Mickey practically mauled John when we got to the door of their house. "Man, oh man, I can't believe you won the championship!" Mickey yelled in his face when he pulled the door open. "Your picture's on the front of the newspaper and everything!"

John bobbed and weaved. "I still have nationals next week."

"You'll kill 'em," Mickey said.

Mrs. Landis appeared behind Mickey. She looked

ghastly, like she hadn't slept in weeks. There were monstrous dark circles under her eyes, which were almost blood-red.

"Come in, please," Mrs. Landis said, her voice raspy and hoarse.

John almost immediately tore up the stairs with Mickey, while Mrs. Landis and Mom talked. I listened to the beginning of the conversation and then decided I really didn't want to hear any more and went upstairs to help John look for the airplane glue.

Mark was in very bad shape. He slept nearly all the time, and he hadn't eaten any solid food in several days. Mickey didn't know it was that bad. At least not yet.

I found the two of them rummaging madly through the closet when I got to the bedroom.

"So why're we lookin' for old airplane glue?" I heard Mickey's muffled voice yell from one end of the closet.

"Just find it!" John yelled back from the other end of the long closet. "I'll tell you later!"

I joined in the search. I looked in drawers at the desk, along the window sill, on the top shelves in the closet. Nothing. Then I had an idea. They always built their airplanes on the bed. So maybe if I pulled the bed out and looked behind it?

"Yeah!" I shouted quite loudly as I spied an empty tube of the airplane glue wedged behind the bed where one of the twins had obviously discarded it.

John and Mickey appeared an instant later. "Did you find one?" John asked, his face flushed from the frantic search.

"Yeah, I did," I said, turning the tube over in my hands to look at the back panel. I scanned the list of ingredients. John and Mickey looked over my shoulders.

"There it is!" John yelled in one ear.

"What?" Mickey asked. "What are we looking for?"

"Benzene!" John yelled again. "There it is!"

Sure enough, John was dead right. Benzene was, indeed, one of the ingredients in this glue. Plain as day. In type so small you needed a Sherlock Holmes spyglass to see it.

"Let's go tell Mom," John said excitedly. He grabbed the old tube from my hands.

"What are we telling your mom?" Mickey asked, still confused but plainly caught up in John's enthusiasm.

"About the benzene," John answered even as he was racing down the stairs.

They both got to the living room before I was even halfway down the stairs. John was holding the tube up so Mom could read it when I entered.

"See?" John told her. "It's right there. See it?"

"Not yet," Mom said calmly. "I'm still reading. I'm . . . yes, now, there, I see it. Benzene." Mom looked up. There was that light in her eyes, which I now recognized rather easily. "John. You were right. I don't believe it."

"So can we go to the hospital now?" John insisted. "Can we? Please? So I can talk to the doctors? Tell them about this?"

"John, shouldn't we explain your theory to Mrs. Landis here first?" Mom said, glancing between her son, me, Mickey, and Mrs. Landis.

"Can't we talk about it on the way to the hospital?" John offered. "Please?"

Mrs. Landis looked over at my mom. "It'll only take me a second to get ready," she said after only a moment's hesitation. "I was planning to go back to the hospital soon anyway."

"Great!" John exclaimed. "We'll wait in the car."

Mom sighed. "No, John, we'll wait right here for Mrs. Landis to get ready. You can sit still for that long."

John almost rebelled. But he was clearly too excited to spoil it by getting angry, so he turned, instead, toward Mrs. Landis. "Can you hurry?"

Mrs. Landis smiled for the first time that morning. "Yes, John, I'll hurry."

"All right," John said, nodding. "Because there's no time to lose."

Mom explained John's theory on the way over to the hospital. Mrs. Landis didn't say much as Mom explained it, with John adding things every other word.

I figured Mrs. Landis had pretty much given up. It seemed so hopeless. The doctors, she said, were willing to try a bone marrow transplant, but unless they knew what was causing the bone marrow failure, the transplant would do no good.

"But don't you see?" John asked her at one point on the drive over. "It's the benzene in the glue. That's it. That's the problem."

"I don't know," Mrs. Landis answered, her voice full of the pain she felt.

"And, in one of the books I read, it said that once you know it's benzene, you can do something about it," John persisted.

"We'll see," Mom said. "Let's just talk to the doctors first."

John practically dragged Mom through the halls of the hospital. I'd never seen him so excited. He was so sure he was right. Well, maybe he was. Only he and Mickey could have known that Mark had been eating the glue. John had found the benzene in the books. And I'd seen it on the back of that tube for myself. So maybe . . .

Mrs. Landis asked the nurse if one of the doctors

who'd been attending her son could join us. We waited in the patient lobby while the nurse paged him.

Two doctors arrived a few minutes later. Mrs. Landis recognized one of them, a Dr. Steve Roberts. The other, Dr. Nathan Hunter, must have been a friend. Both of them also wore badges that read "pediatric oncologist." *Both words John might have to spell next week at the national spelling bee,* I thought ruefully.

Mrs. Landis and Mom explained, briefly, why they were there. The two doctors were attentive, but slightly bored. They'd heard a million theories from worried parents. This was just one more tall tale.

Finally, John couldn't stand it any longer. He started tugging on one of the doctors' white lab coats. "Doctor!" he said plaintively. "In *The Merck Manual,* it says that benzene can cause aplastic anemia."

Dr. Hunter looked down at John. "Eh, what's that, son?" he said easily.

"The Merck Manual, it says . . ."

"You read that manual?" Dr. Hunter interjected, amused.

"Yes, I've read it," John said impatiently. "And it says benzene can cause what's making Mark sick."

"Is that so?" Dr. Hunter said, his eyebrows slightly raised.

John got that faraway look in his eyes. "Exposure to certain chemical agents like benzene . . . can result in aplastic anemia," he intoned, remembering the passage from the manual.

"You have a pretty good memory, son," Dr. Hunter marveled. "And, yes, I do recall that benzene poisoning can cause aplastic anemia."

John held up the empty tube of model airplane glue proudly. "Well, there's benzene in this glue. And Mark eats it all the time. He likes the taste. It's how he gets rid of it when it squishes out. Mickey and I have seen him do it all the time."

Dr. Hunter glanced over at the other doctor sharply. He grabbed the tube from John, turned it over and read the ingredient list. A visible look of shock crossed his face. He passed the tube over to Dr. Roberts, who also looked at it.

"You say Mark regularly ingests this kind of glue?" Dr. Roberts asked John.

"Yep, he eats it," Mickey said. John just nodded in agreement.

The two doctors looked at each other. Dr. Hunter was the first to speak. "This would explain the sudden onset."

"It sure would," Dr. Roberts mused.

"We could run some tests to make sure he isn't still transferring benzene into his marrow," Dr. Hunter said.

"And we can begin the whole blood transfusions immediately. It also means a bone marrow transplant from Mickey is almost sure to do the trick, once we know the benzene is gone," Dr. Roberts mused.

Dr. Roberts then turned. "Nurse!" he called out sharply. "Can I have the charts on Mark Landis, please?" He turned back to his colleague. "You know, if we start the transfusions right now, we can probably have him ready for surgery in a few days."

Dr. Hunter knelt down, so his eyes were level with John's. "You know, son," he said softly, "this may just work. Thank you. How did you ever think to look for this?"

John didn't flinch. He looked the doctor right in the eye. "I wasn't looking for anything in particular. I just read everything I could find. This just kind of jumped out at me."

"Well, if this works, thank God it did," Dr. Hunter said, shaking his head. "We'd never have known about the benzene, otherwise. We didn't know what to look for. But you did."

----❷❹

"So are you ready?" I asked John the following Saturday, the morning of the national spelling bee championship.

"Yeah, sure," he shrugged.

"Are you nervous?"

"Not really."

"Don't you want to win?"

"Um, sure, why not," John answered nonchalantly.

I smiled to myself. John was ready. Win or lose, he was ready.

You see, something had happened to John. There was no mistaking it now. No matter what happened, he wasn't about to drop out of elementary school. No way. Not now. Dropping out of school was the farthest thing from his mind.

Over the course of the week, John had spent every spare moment at the hospital, beside Mark's bed. That's where he studied for the national spelling bee championship, mostly. Not that he needed to study all that much.

They *had* found traces of benzene still lingering in Mark's system, but not enough to do him much more harm. They'd pumped lots of whole blood through him. And, by the weekend, he was well enough that they were able to schedule a bone marrow transplant operation.

You see, it turned out, with identical twins, a bone marrow transplant can work. Mickey was so excited he could hardly stand it. He wasn't worried at all that he'd have to go into the hospital for an operation too. He just wanted to help his brother.

They scheduled the operation on the Friday before John went to the national spelling bee finals. Thanks to the whole blood transfusions and some forced nourishment, Mark was much more alert. The doctors were very optimistic, now, that he could recover.

It was all I could do to keep John from just skipping the spelling championship altogether. He really wanted to be at the hospital. He wanted to make absolutely sure that it all had worked out.

It wasn't until I finally convinced him that it would be weeks before they could be certain that Mark's fragile bone marrow had recovered from the toxic poison and that the addition of Mickey's bone marrow had helped too, that John agreed to go to the bee.

But his mind was still clearly intent on just one thing. And it wasn't the spelling bee.

But, you know what, I didn't care. Neither did Mom. There was a fire raging in John's soul. Neither of us had ever seen it before. He had focus, direction, a purpose. He had a very faint glimmer of what his mind was capable of. And he wanted to use it in the worst way. Or the best way, I mean. I was now sure he would.

It was funny. Once upon a time, when our father ruled our family with an iron fist and an alcohol-induced rage, every child under his thumb was afraid to try anything.

We reflected our father's unwillingness to believe in the human soul and spirit. We were afraid to try. We were uncertain about what we might accomplish. He was a coward and, by his presence, so were we.

It was only when our mother was brave enough to leave him finally that we, his children, were able to find our wings as well.

I had taken up tennis and won a national championship. And now John was poised to try his hand at a different kind of national championship. Neither of us would have made the attempt within our dad's awful presence.

My belief and trust in God had happened despite my dad. Every day away from my father, my deep anger against him subsided. And my hope for the future grew.

The ride to the spelling championship this time was a short one. They held the nationals in downtown Washington, which was about a half-hour away from the suburbs in northern Virginia.

Our family was unusually quiet on the ride in. We all wished John well. We all wanted him to succeed, yet none of us were really sure what might happen.

John seemed the least concerned by any of this. He seemed oblivious to pressure.

Because John had been so preoccupied with the Landis twins, we'd skipped all of the fun and festivities that went along with the national spelling bee championships.

All the other families of the state champions did fun things like tour the White House and Congress. They visited the Smithsonian and the National Air and Space Museum. They got to sit through a Supreme Court session.

John didn't seem to mind, though. Mom had asked him about all of it and he'd just said no, he wanted to stay close by Mark and Mickey, his friends. Mom didn't argue much.

The championship was held in the small Constitution Hall auditorium. There were swarms of local reporters everywhere, who'd traveled to Washington to cover their state champions. It was like a carnival in the hall.

We found a little corner of the hall to ourselves and said our good-byes to John, who had to go backstage for a briefing before the championship began.

I grabbed John right before he left.

"Now, you know you're ready for this, right?" I asked him.

John nodded. Only now was the fear and the realization of what he was about to do beginning to creep into his eyes.

"And you know that you only have to do your best here, right? That's all. Nothing more, nothing less than your best?"

"I know," John said in a small voice.

"You're already a champion, John," I tried to say with confidence. "Don't forget that."

"Thanks, Cally," he told me. "I mean, for everything."

I smiled and shoved him towards the stage. "Go blow their doors off, OK?"

John shoved his glasses up higher on his nose and then turned to make his way backstage. *He'd do just fine,* I thought. *Just fine.*

The 50 state champions came onstage five minutes later and took their seats across the stage, in a long, single row. I couldn't help but notice that John sure did look a lot smaller than the rest.

Not surprisingly, because all of these kids could spell like crazy, no one dropped out in the first round. They breezed through all 50 kids and then plunged into round two.

John stepped up to the mike about a third of the way through this second round. A few kids had already dropped out ahead of him in this round. His word was "anent." As usual, I'd never heard of it before. What's more, I didn't entirely understand how the dumb word was used.

John looked a little confused onstage. Then he spelled it with some hesitation. "A-n-e-n," he said right away. Then he paused for a long time, maybe thirty seconds. "S—and then t," he said at last.

The judges conferred briefly. "I'm sorry, that is incorrect," the judge said. "There is no 's' in the word."

John stood at the microphone, clearly in shock. He didn't believe it. He did not think he had misspelled the word. I could see that he was frozen in place.

The judges could see that too. "Go on, son," one of them said gently. "You've misspelled a word. We need to move on to the next contestant."

But still John didn't move. He was obviously wrestling with something. I could see his mind racing, even from here. He tried to speak. Nothing came out. He cleared his throat and tried again. "Could, um, could you please check that?" he managed at last.

The judge who'd told him he'd misspelled the word glanced down at his own book briefly and then looked back up. "Your spelling of the word was incorrect, son. There is no 's' in the word."

John held his ground. He still didn't believe it. The crowd was beginning to murmur and rustle. "I . . . I think that maybe there are two spellings," he said, his voice cracking just a little.

The judges glanced at each other. The first judge showed the others the place in his book where "anent" was spelled. They all nodded in agreement. The first judge spoke again. "No, I'm sorry, but you have spelled the word incorrectly," he said more firmly. "Now, please, exit the stage. We need to move on."

"Could you please check it against the official dictionaries?" John asked quickly. "Please?"

The judges hesitated. This was so irregular. Was there precedent for going to the dictionaries?

"Give the kid a break!" someone yelled from the crowd.

"Yeah, check the dictionary for the kid!" someone else yelled.

It seemed the judges had no choice. There would be open rebellion if they didn't check now. So one of the judges walked offstage quickly and, a moment later, returned with three different dictionaries in hand.

Three judges looked simultaneously. Two of the judges closed their books right away, clearly satisfied that there was no second spelling in theirs.

But the third judge lingered for a little while in his dictionary. None of us could see what kind it was. But the third judge then gathered the others together, and there was heated debate for nearly a minute.

And then the first judge, the one who'd tried to whisk John off the stage, said, "It, uh, it seems that you are correct, son. In the *American Heritage Dictionary,* there is, indeed, a second *very rare* spelling of the word that includes an 's,' just as you have spelled it."

The crowd applauded spontaneously, nearly drowning out his final comments that the judges had decided to award him with a correct spelling of the word. I had to marvel. That was, of course, the dictionary we had at home.

Our family, of course, went bonkers. One moment John had been out, and now he was back in. We ignored the funny stares of the other families near us.

The incident seemed to light a fire that had been dormant in John. For the next three rounds, as kids started to fall one by one, John stepped up to the microphone with confidence and spelled the words without even asking for them to be used in a sentence. None of the other kids were doing that, but John was clearly off in a different dimension now.

After nearly two hours, they finally took a break. There were just three kids remaining—John, another boy at least as small as him from Pennsylvania, and a thin, hawkish girl from New York.

During the break, they moved all the chairs offstage, save the three remaining for the final contestants. John hurried offstage to join us.

"Great job!" Jana said, giving him a quick hug. Karen joined in the hug. John looked thoroughly embarrassed. Chris and I contented ourselves with high fives, which John very nearly missed. He caught just one of Chris' fingers and only two of mine. Oh well.

"I was proud of you for standing up for what you thought was right on that word," Mom said to him.

"Yeah, that was cool," Jana added.

I was curious about one thing, though. "Why didn't you just give the normal spelling, instead of the rare one?"

John gave me a blank stare. "I don't know. I just remembered both of them. I didn't know which was which."

"Seats, please!" one of the judges called out, trying to silence the commotion in the hall. John waved and then hurried back to his seat.

It wasn't until he was back onstage, sitting in only one of the three remaining chairs, that it finally dawned on me. John could actually win this thing! It was really, truly possible.

The other two, though, looked quite formidable. They too had appeared quite confident through the earlier rounds, especially the girl from New York.

They went through the next rounds briskly. Each of them spelled words correctly through one round, two rounds, three rounds. It wasn't until the seventh round that the boy from Pennsylvania finally stumbled on "dumortierite," which sounded like a mineral of some sort used to make porcelain. The boy left out the "i" after the first "t."

And then there were just two. They stopped the competition briefly to remove the third chair from the stage.

I was so nervous I finally decided to get out of my chair and take a walk. I told Mom where I was going and then headed for the back of the auditorium briskly.

I almost ran smack into Dr. Burnley. I was walking up the aisle with my head down. I looked up and there she was, leaning casually against the back of the auditorium.

"Oh, hi, you came," I said, trying to keep the look of astonishment from showing on my face.

Dr. Burnley smiled. "Yes, Cally, I came. I told you I would, and I try to keep my word."

We looked at each other for a long moment, as if we were the only two people in the world. I so much wanted to ask her why she was here, why she'd taken a special interest in John's case.

As if reading my mind, Dr. Burnley smiled a second time. "I was held back too when I was John's age," she said. "I never forgot it. I was so angry at everyone, it almost ruined my life. There was no one around to explain it to me at the time. I had to figure it out on my own."

"Oh," was all I could manage to say.

"John's lucky," she added, glancing up at the stage.

"Why's that?" I asked.

"He has you, and the rest of his family. That's all that matters, you know."

I nodded. I understood, at last. And I agreed with her. "Yes, I think I know that."

Dr. Burnley looked away. I could see a slight mistiness in her eyes. "Go on," she said harshly. "Your family's probably looking for you."

I turned to head back down the aisle to our seats. "Thanks, Dr. Burnley," I called out over one shoulder. "Really. Thanks a lot."

"Part of the job," she answered back, but I knew her heart wasn't in it. Not in that answer, I mean. I knew, now, where her real heart was.

The rest of the "crew" was on the edge of their seats when I returned. The competition was about to begin again. Only Susan ignored the obvious tension in the air. She'd found a friend to play with and was now thoroughly ignoring the contest.

"Do it," Chris pleaded silently.

"Come on, John," Jana said, all eight of her fingers crossed.

Mom's face was a grim mask. I reached over and nudged her a little. "It's okay. He'll win. Don't worry," I said. Mom just shook her head. She didn't believe.

The two contestants battled back and forth through another six rounds, neither of them hesitating over a word. The girl from New York appeared especially self-confident. Her knowledge seemed endless.

Yet I was confident of John's memory. If he'd actually seen the word somewhere, at some time, he would remember it. I was certain of that. It was the word he hadn't seen that I was worried about.

Which finally happened, of course. In the eighth round between the final two, John got a word he'd never seen before. I could tell by the crestfallen look on his face as the judge pronounced it. "The word is 'hypocorism.'"

I don't know why John had never seen this word, when he'd seen all the others. But he clearly had not seen this one.

Yet I could also see that John had learned something. He began to spell the word slowly, by phonetics and roots. He spelled the first four letters, the next three and, finally, the last three.

"Correct," the judge said. John almost wilted. He had guessed right! He was wobbly as he returned to his chair.

It was only a matter of time. The girl from New York finally got a word she'd never heard before — "rhizome," which sounded like a root growing underground.

The girl naturally spelled it the way many of the words like this sound, with an "rhy" at the beginning. But she had guessed wrong, though none of us knew that until the judge said so.

She immediately burst into tears. She stood there at the microphone, tears streaming down her face. Then, with a sob, she collapsed in her chair. She refused to even look up as John stepped to the microphone.

"R-h-y-s-o-m-e," John said quickly, not even looking at the judges.

"I'm sorry, that too is incorrect," the judge said. "The contest continues." There was a gasp from the crowd.

I watched John carefully as he returned to his seat, but not before he gave the girl an affectionate pat on the shoulder. The girl had stopped sobbing. There was now a radiant, ecstatic smile on her face. She couldn't believe her good fortune.

I *knew* John had deliberately misspelled that word. But why? Why would he do such a thing? It made no sense at all. None.

Three rounds later, John again misspelled a word. He did so quickly, efficiently, and then returned to his seat. He watched in silence as his opponent spelled his word correctly, then spelled her own word for the national championship.

When the judge confirmed that she was correct and that she had won the contest, she thrust her fists high in the air and let out a terrible yell of victory. It almost sounded like a screech. It echoed through the hall.

John held out his hand to congratulate the girl. The girl ignored it, choosing instead to clench her fists and shake them briefly in John's face and then at the crowd to celebrate her victory. The girl's family and friends rushed to the stage, mobbing her. There were now tears of joy streaming down the girl's face.

There was a funny, wistful smile on John's face as he drifted away from the mad scene, toward the edge of the stage. There was no mob of reporters rushing to surround John now, only our family.

"Tough luck, John," Chris said.

"You gave it your best shot," Karen said, beaming.

"We're all proud of you, John," Mom said, giving John a huge hug, which he gladly returned.

I didn't say anything. I was pretty certain John had lost on purpose. What I still could not understand was why.

I turned to look back at the stage, where the girl was still squealing with delight over her victory. And then I knew. I knew.

John had never entered the contest to win. He'd

entered it to redeem himself, to prove to himself and the world that he wasn't stupid, that he wasn't a moron or an imbecile.

And, having proved that, he chose not to win. He chose to let that go to someone else. It was a decision I could not have made. Very few could make such a decision. Very few had John's unique gift and, now, his unique ability to use it.

But there weren't many like John to begin with. Of that, I was certain.

"John, you're one of a kind," I said with a chuckle to no one in particular in the rapidly thinning auditorium.

I looked over at my younger brother. He caught my eye, inclined his head toward the mob scene on the stage, and then rolled his eyes.

"Next year," I called to him.

"Next year," he agreed.

Then we both laughed.